Also by Doc Macomber

(The Jack Vu Mysteries)

The Killer Coin

Wolf's Remedy

Snip

Riff Raff

(The Jason Colefield Mysteries)

River City

River Rat

River Rat

(A Jason Colefield Mystery)

By

Doc Macomber

Floating Word Press, LLC
Portland, Oregon

Floating Word Press, LLC
1017 SW Morrison St. Suite 215
Portland, Oregon 97205

Library of Congress Control Number: 2017918588

Soft Cover ISBN: 978-1-941297--05-6

COVER DESIGNED BY DIVERSITY DESIGN STUDIOS
Editor: Martha Cowen
Author photograph Copyright © 2014 by Ty Hitzemann
Cover photograph Copyright © 2017 by Doc Haake Productions

Manufactured in the United States of America

Printing Number

987654321

First Edition

For my good buds, Brent Stowe & Dave Huitt.

I'll miss you guys…

1

The dream came to him like some dreams do, quirky, rattling, disjointed. This one featured a big fish, a brute of a salmon, which rose out of the depths of the river and swallowed him. He struggled and fought his way free — slimy, fear-struck, damaged yet temporarily safe, or so he thought. Then one of his neighbors shot what sounded like a gun, leaving him fired up and dealing with his PTSD. He forced himself to breathe in slowly before he sprang into action. His VA counselor would be proud.

Before that Deputy Jason Colefield had been trying to enjoy his day off. Staring at the rolling Willamette River, fishing, and musing about how to coax his ex, Jill, back into his life had become a familiar routine.

"Hi there, neighbor!" The voice startled him.

Tall, long-legged and nimble, a smiling woman sauntered across the deck juggling two bottles of beer. Her tank top had the words "Boy Beater" emblazoned across the front. Her shoulder-length dark hair was pulled back. Gold earrings sparkled in the sunlight. As he straightened up, he noticed another bikini clad stranger next door holding a foaming bottle of champagne, whose cork was probably the source of the noise he'd mistaken for a gunshot.

"Hope we're not disturbing you."

He arched his brow sarcastically.

She glanced at his fishing rod. "Any luck?"

"Not yet. But that's the funny thing about luck, it can always change."

The remark stopped her for a moment. He struggled out of his deck chair and stuck out his hand. "Deputy Jason Colefield at your service."

She handed off a beer, her broadening grin revealing a slight gap between her front teeth. Colefield found it oddly attractive.

"Doctor Nicole Dafoe. Pleased to meet you, Deputy Colefield." They clinked bottles. She wasn't wearing a ring.

"So, you're my new neighbor?"

"Yes, though at the moment I haven't a lot of furniture. In fact, I haven't a lot of anything…"

"Sounds like you're starting over?"

"Yes, in some ways." Her smile wandered. She squinted at the sun's reflection on the blue-gray expanse. "I think everybody deserves a second chance. Don't you?"

Colefield nodded, his mind drifting to Jill.

Nicole became distracted as a swarm of pesky gnats surrounded them. "It's this perfume. It was a housewarming gift." She glanced down and smirked. "As was this tasteful shirt … I wonder which attracted these pests."

Colefield liked her wit and her spicy scent. Apparently, this meant that he and the bugs had the same taste.

He changed the subject. "So, you must own the gold Mercedes 450 SL convertible in the parking lot?"

She nodded. "A classic and sturdy. I like that in my cars and relationships."

"I drive a 1974 Ford pickup for the same reason."

They chit-chatted about various subjects just allowing the conversation to flow. Colefield studied her profile. She was striking in her own unique way. Her voice was soothing. Words floated from her lips like cottonwood puffs drifting by on a summer day.

As the river breeze shifted ashore, Colefield got another whiff of her perfume. She smiled at him but became self-conscious and stepped back.

"I've got too much on, don't I?"

"Are you referring to your cologne?"

"Cute." She gestured toward the party. "My colleagues are full of surprises. I was counting on housewares: plates, utensils. Instead, they bring me bottles of perfume, a 'Boy Beater' top, a book with tips on cooking in the nude, and apparently, they have signed me up for a website called 'Singledocs.com'."

"So, what kind of doctor are you?"

"I'm a witch doctor." She grinned.

"Are you any good at it?"

She laughed. "I'll cast a spell on you and conjure up fresh fish for dinner." She finished her beer and glanced over at the fishing rod. "May I?"

"By all means."

She put her bottle down by her feet and picked up the rod. She held it firmly, examining it like she'd handled a few in her life. "I just moved to Portland. I'm a psychiatrist and work at the VA hospital."

"Maybe I'll see you up there sometime."

"Why? Feeling crazy?"

Colefield could see she regretted the words as soon as they were out. He shrugged. "I'm a Navy veteran in a new program called 'Shock Talk' where we learn to control adrenaline stress reactions to situations we witness or intuit. Kind of brain waves meet meditation."

"Interesting. Humans intuit things constantly. How do you know which ones to ignore?"

"Basic goal is 'reflect before you react'. Its intention is to help us control our PTSD over memories or circumstances we can't change."

Nicole's irises enlarged. "How long have you been in law enforcement?"

"Ten years."

Her lips opened as if she wanted to respond then thought better of it.

"Something you wanted to say?"

She glanced down at her empty bottle. "Would you have any tequila?"

"Coming right up." Colefield took both bottles and set them down by the back door of the houseboat and went inside.

A large bank of windows offered a good view of the deck. Nicole proved to be interesting. She could handle herself. Running out some leaded line from the reel, hooking her small index finger over the filament, she raised the pole, arched her back and made a splendid cast like an old pro toward the center of the river.

Colefield felt a tug at his heart...

The moment didn't last. Eighty-five-year-old former Marine Captain William A. Montgomery hobbled down the spiral staircase scowling, bare-chested, in sagging jockey shorts. He was packing a M82 sniper rifle.

"What brings you to my humble abode?" Montgomery barked. "Here to pay rent?"

Colefield pointed out the window. Montgomery turned and his disposition immediately improved. He admired the lovely visage of curvaceous flesh fishing off his deck. And then as if on cue, she reeled in the line, back arched, giving both men a full profile of her physique.

"Well, you might want to say hello to our new neighbor after you've put on some pants."

"Our new what?"

Commanding an artillery unit and forty-plus years as an NRA instructor had pretty much destroyed any hope of Montgomery hearing anything less than a mortar round.

"Our new neighbor in slip 13."

"Is this the mermaid on my deck?"

"Yes."

"Why is she holding your rod?"

"She's waiting for Tequila..."

"That's my kind of woman."

"Which is why I need to raid your liquor cabinet." Colefield moved back from the window. He eased the barrel of the sniper rifle aside. "What are you planning on doing with that?"

"Depends."

"This isn't about the Mayor again?"

Montgomery glanced at his old Timex watch. "At fifteen-thirty, the little bastard is riding his bicycle across the Sellwood Bridge to meet with park officials. They're up to no good. Consider it target practice."

Colefield shook his head in disbelief. "Where do you keep the tequila?

"Who's Sheila?"

"I said — tequila."

"It's beneath the kitchen counter. But it's locked."

"You're locking up your booze now?"

Montgomery put the rifle down by his side. "Got to! Housekeeper's a lush."

Colefield made his way over to the cabinet. A heavy-duty chain secured the doors. Both handles fastened by a WWII vintage five-pound padlock that looked like it would dissuade even the most die-hard drunk. Montgomery wore the key around his neck along with his dog tags. Begrudgingly, he removed the cheap chain and handed it to Colefield. After Colefield got the lock open, he removed a half-gallon jug of cut-rate tequila and started to relock the cabinet.

"Hey!" Montgomery shouted. "Aren't you forgetting something?"

"Starting happy hour early?"

"Does a bear shit in the woods? Fetch my Pusser's."

"I promised your son I'd keep an eye on you."

"You would profit more keeping an eye on that vivacious dame outside. By the way, do those mammary mountaintops come with a name?"

"Nicole Dafoe. And I believe she's single."

"Single begets trouble!"

"She's also a witch doctor."

"That begets double trouble! This may be an interesting summer after all. Is she any good with a Glock?"

Colefield reached in and pawed through the liquor bottles until he found the squatty rum bottle with the British navy blue and gold label. He pulled it out and placed it down on the counter beside the tequila.

"I suspect lad, with her marvelous wiles, she could throw us and blow us before we could lick her and dick her."

Colefield winced. "You want me to lock this?"

"Leave it. It'll be a test to see how steady my hands are after I take potshots at the Mayor and his buddies."

Colefield carried the half-gallon bottle of tequila out the back door. Over his shoulder, he noticed Montgomery's grizzled face pressed against the window watching Nicole.

As he approached his new neighbor with the bottle, she turned and flashed him a smile.

"It's not top shelf, but it should do."

"It's generous. I appreciate it very much," she said. "Shall we trade?" she held out the fishing rod.

They made the exchange — a fishing pole for a long pull from a half-gallon jug of very cheap tequila. She didn't flinch a bit downing the rot-gut liquor.

"The owner inside gloating is William A. Montgomery. You have him to thank for the booze. I live in his small houseboat out front — 12A."

She turned and waved to Montgomery, who pressed his pelvis against the glass and enthusiastically waved back in his jockey shorts.

"He seems like a real gentleman."

"He is anything but…"

"Well, if it's not too much trouble I may just have to keep this. Would that be OK? I've got some thirsty party guests."

"Montgomery still has a stockpile from Prohibition. He won't miss it. But let me take a pull before you abscond with it."

But before Colefield could take a drink, he saw a tug at the end of the rod. A fish hit. A big fish. He reared back hoping he'd set the hook in time.

Nicole jumped with excitement. "I told you I was a witch doctor."

He let out some line to keep the fish from snapping the tip of the rod and worked it. Sweat streamed down his face. After a long fight, he reeled a thirty-pound Chinook onto the deck.

He dropped the keeper near their feet and they both hopped back as the tired fish swatted its powerful tail back and forth like a machete. Colefield plucked the half-gallon bottle of tequila from Nicole's hand before she could object or cover her eyes and in one heavy blow whacked the salmon on the head.

He passed the jug back to his new neighbor like nothing had happened. She smiled and glanced down at the fish again. "Marvelous!"

Perhaps because of the excitement next door, several of Nicole's guests walked out and stood on the balcony. They looked over and smiled, holding up empty glasses.

Nicole held up the bottle of tequila.

Another woman stepped out onto the deck, spotted her friend and strolled over.

"Grace, meet my neighbor, Deputy Jason Colefield."

"Hello, deputy." Grace touched Nicole's arm. "We're about to have a toast and we've run out of alcohol."

Nicole nodded and turned to Colefield. "I've got to run. Hey — if you're in the mood to share a salmon dinner later, just say the word."

"You're on."

She jumped over the gap between the two decks then stopped. While her friend wandered off ahead, she faced Colefield.

"You ever do bodyguard work?" she asked quietly.

"Is it for you or somebody else?"

"We'll chat about it later." She turned to go. "Thanks again for the tequila."

Colefield contemplated her request, consciously trying to prevent various violent scenarios from preying on his mind. After the moment passed, he picked up his trophy by the gills, humming the tune "Afternoon Delight."

2

He had just dumped the salmon on the galley counter when he heard a knock on the patio door. He wiped his hands dry and headed toward it.

There was a tall thin man standing on his deck, shirtless, wearing surfer shorts and flip-flops. Colefield noticed some grease smudges on his hands.

"Hey, Bernie, what's up?"

"Can you give me a hand? Got a little issue with the boat again."

"Sure."

He closed the door and followed his neighbor to the slip down on the end. Bernie owned a 1960 Custom Skagit 14' runabout. The turquoise paint alone was enough to make the boat stand out. It also had center console steering with pedestal seating and a canvas fisherman's top. It was powered by a very finicky Evinrude 2-stroke outboard.

But the boat was not in its slip.

"Where's your runabout?"

Bernie pointed downstream. The brightly colored boat was tied off to a tree along the riverbank at the end of the moorage.

"What's it doing there?"

"It died and won't start."

"Let's go take a look."

They walked up the ramp to the parking lot, walked to the end, and then hiked down to the boat. Someone had removed the engine cover and had pulled off the plug wire.

"Just turns over and over."

"Does it have gas?"

"Filled the tank yesterday."

"Is it getting fuel?"

"Smells like it."

"What's the plug wire doing off?"

"I was getting ready to pull the plug."

There was an open toolbox by the stern with a collection of wrenches and screwdrivers. Colefield climbed into the boat. What he thought might just be a quick fix turned into a job that lasted for hours. He was greasy and sweaty. He'd tried every trick in the book. Nothing worked. It had spark and then it didn't. It'd fire and then it wouldn't. It had to be electrical. In the end, he had fetched Montgomery's Boston Whaler and towed the boat back to Bernie's slip.

As the sky took on a ruby glow, he realized that he'd probably missed a dinner opportunity with Nicole.

"Shit, I got to go, Bernie. I think you need a new coil. Get one tomorrow and I'll give you a hand with it after work."

Back at his place, he figured first things first. Deal with the fish on the kitchen counter. Then go see if the girls were still interested in a barbecue.

He entered the galley and after swatting a few flies away from the carcass, he looked through the drawers until he found a suitable knife to fillet the salmon. There was plenty of meat on the bone. Enough to feed Nicole's guests and then some...

He slid the edge of the sharp blade under the gills and ran it down the length of the body stopping before he reached the tailfin, then gutted it, sliced off the head and set it outside on his galley windowsill for Calico Jack, a feral cat who had adopted him last winter.

He cut the fish into thirds, stowed the works in Ziplocs in the refrigerator next to a partial six-pack of Heineken and cleaned up.

At the moment there wasn't much he could do to improve his appearance. He felt and looked rough. His Irish-red hair was a mess and his T-shirt and shorts were filthy and wrinkled.

To hell with it, he thought. He was probably too late anyway.

Despite his appearance and stale breath, he walked down the narrow passageway between the two houseboats and banged on their back door. The music had been silenced, as had the laughter and the lights.

He looked in through the glass and didn't see any movement. He tried again and after no response, he sat down and stared at the city lights downriver, thinking about what to do next.

He thought he caught a scent of Nicole's perfume lingering in the night air but assumed it was just his imagination. Nonetheless, he felt compelled to check the parking lot for the Mercedes just to be sure.

It was quiet out, the sky clear with a full moon. Up in the parking lot the gold convertible was gone, as he'd predicted.

Since he had nothing else to do, he figured he'd check on Montgomery before returning home. Nicole might have left word with him before leaving. At times, he was a hopeful optimist...

He found Montgomery in the galley, slumped in a wheelchair, holding his sniper rifle across his lap, his snowy white head tilted back, snoring like a trumpeter. On the dining table lay the cap from the bottle of Pusser's Rum and the bottle looked empty. The sterling silver goblet from which Montgomery liked to drink his daily ration of rum had a dead fly floating in the bottom. There seemed no reason to wake him if he could pry the rifle from his grip, which he did without protest.

Colefield set the rifle aside, pleased that it had not been fired, turned off the overhead lights, and then returned to the tender. As he was walking through his front door he heard his cell phone ring.

* * *

Colefield was still playing the telephone conversation back in his mind as he pulled his old pickup into the darkened parking lot of the Multnomah County River Patrol. He climbed out and headed inside feeling a little dehydrated from the drinks he had earlier that afternoon. Diving in the middle of the night was about the last thing he expected he'd be doing on his day off. Body recovery was never pleasant, day or night.

The door was unlocked and the lights were on. Deputy Bart had already arrived ahead of him. The young deputy was standing by a window with the marine radio microphone in hand, looking out at the river. He wore a grim expression while focusing on the tense voice bellowing through the radio's tiny speaker.

Colefield had seen that look before. The "kid" as Colefield liked to think of him, had grown up on a dairy farm outside of Eugene and spent most of his time milking cows, not perfecting his poker face. He once told Colefield that keeping all the milking machines running fixated him on two things, mechanics and tits. Colefield didn't know how the boob fixation was working out, but he was the glue that kept the machines running at the River Patrol. He also brought enthusiasm to internet searches, which drove Colefield crazy. He was a big guy with a good heart. He would go far within the department if he hung in there.

"I'll get my dive gear," Colefield told him and started to walk off down the hall.

"Weaver and the Lieutenant are already at the scene. They have a visual on sonar."

"Where'd the car go in?"

"Near the I-205 Bridge."

"Any survivors?"

"They don't know yet."

"What about witnesses?"

"A security guard from the Port of Portland called it in."

Colefield grabbed a bottle of water from the cooler in the locker room, chugged it down, and lobbed the empty across the room like launching a small missile. The bottle caught the lip of the trash can and went skidding across the floor. Colefield squelched the feeling that he wasn't on his game tonight.

After he lugged his dive gear out of the building and down the Gleason Boat Ramp, he slammed open the boathouse door at the end of the dock. Bart was doing what he'd asked — checking the fuel tank in the sled because he couldn't remember if Weaver had filled it on Tuesday. They'd made a run upriver near the Bonneville Dam in search of a Catalina that reportedly had gone aground east of Camas near Reed Island. They hadn't topped off the tanks when they returned, because Weaver was running late for his kid's softball game. Said he'd handle it later. Colefield figured it was prudent to check.

He walked over and dumped his gear in the bow of the jet boat, untied the lines and climbed aboard.

Bart fired up the engine and backed the aluminum boat out of the covered moorage. Time was passing...

He gunned it, dodging flotsam while the sled splashed its way upriver. Colefield knew Bart loved the sway and movement of the boat as it battled current, wind and weather, never happier than when he arrived at a site soaked to the skin. Meanwhile, Colefield focused on organizing his scuba gear. Lieutenant Briggs called on the radio. Where the hell were they?

Despite the circumstances, the breeze off the Columbia River felt invigorating. There was no fog to speak of. And with the exception of a 5-knot east wind kicking up some sand along the jagged shoreline and blowing in a fine mist of invisible grit, the conditions seemed favorable for a dive. And having a full moon would help with visibility.

Sections of the dark island were ablaze in light, as was Government Island farther upriver. Since the Fourth of July was days away, everywhere you looked folks were setting off fireworks early. As the boat passed, someone lit off a bottle rocket that shot out over the river and lit up a section of the water.

The noise and commotion was distracting tonight. Colefield was trying to concentrate on the job ahead. Farther south the control tower lights of Portland International Airport beaconed in the sky.

Colefield could see a police car with lights flashing, mid-point along the shoulder of the I-205 Bridge, and more flashing lights just west of the bridge along the curvy section of Marine Drive.

The officer standing outside his vehicle on the bridge had a spotlight pointed down on a section of the river, a halo of white looming over the dark water. There were more spotlights along the steep embankment leading down to the water. Several personal watercraft were circling the area. Bart flipped on the siren and flashed the sled's spot on several of the powerboats. They got the message to move.

Colefield spotted the Lieutenant manning the twin screw 32-foot River Patrol boat while Weaver craned his head down toward the water, looking at something in the river. Colefield pointed to Bart to steer in that direction.

The sled glided alongside the other boat. Colefield threw Weaver a line which he caught on the first try and tied off. Already in his dive suit, Weaver looked eager to get this thing underway.

"The wreckage is off our portside!" Weaver shouted.

Colefield stared at the water. The river had too much silt to see anything clearly. He couldn't get a bearing or tell much from there. And the spotlights weren't helping. He read the direction of wind and noticed rippling on the water.

"I'll drop in from the sled and take a cable down. I'll have Bart radio to kill the shore lights."

"Your call, buddy. I'll see you down-under."

The lieutenant poked his head out of the cabin. "I want you guys to harness up," he said. "The dam's open. It's a rolling tide and this makes for one swift mother-fuckin' current."

Colefield studied the shoreline. The embankment where the car had gone over was a good fifty feet or more of vertical drop. Not sheer, but to the person or persons inside the vehicle, it probably wouldn't have felt that way. If the side sonar was working correctly, then the car had to be traveling at very high speed to make it this far out in the river.

He did some more quick calculations. He looked at the depth finder. It appeared from the green glowing dots on the small screen that the car was resting on a ledge of basalt, twenty-five feet below the surface. He figured given where it was the vehicle could shift from one side to the other. Weaver and he would have to calculate their moves precisely.

Bart gave the word and the patrolmen scouting the shoreline turned off their spotlights. A search and rescue unit pulled along the shoulder and parked, followed by a tow truck, and a second emergency response vehicle.

Yeah, he thought, this wasn't the best part of the job. He preferred to think about his new neighbor's gap toothed smile instead.

Colefield put on his scuba tank while Bart cinched up the yellow harness around his waist and handed him an underwater spotlight. Colefield slipped the strap over his shoulder, grabbed the cable and coil of rope and looked over at Weaver who was shoving his regulator into his mouth.

He flashed Weaver thumbs up and disappeared into the murky river.

3

The mind plays tricks on you when you cut off sound and light. Colefield equalized the pressure in his ears as he descended into the cold. He moved his gloved finger over the switch of his underwater light, flipped it on, and then kicked his feet back and forth to slow his movements and fight the current pushing against his chest.

Unidentifiable objects appeared and disappeared at random. He tried to slow his descent, searching for a glimmer from above that his dive buddy was coming.

He made out a darkened silhouette gliding down through the muddy haze and kicked out of his descending path, turning his attention now onto the river bottom where reduced visibility prohibited him from seeing beyond a few feet.

Something caught his eye. Colefield saw a large golden blur resting on the river bottom and figured it was the wreckage.

Weaver thudded onto his shoulder. His partner pointed frantically behind him.

Colefield turned just as a dozen jack salmon swam by — the fish so close that either of them could have reached out and snagged one by the tail. The salmon, Colefield figured, were moving upriver to their spawning grounds beyond the locks, forging ahead toward nature's mystery. And if they were lucky enough to survive, they could fulfill their life's mission. Colefield wondered what his life's mission would turn out to be. So far it hadn't followed any of his planned scripts.

He spotted the wreckage directly below him. The car looked unstable and risky. With the heavy current they were fighting, the vehicle could shift positions at any moment, entangling them in the steel tow cable they had to attach to the undercarriage. Being pinned inside or underneath the chassis was the last thing either of them wanted. But that was not what was troubling him now.

Colefield felt a sense of urgency and swam faster. Using hand-signals he conveyed to his partner to hurry.

A gold Mercedes 450 SL!

Her classic sedan had flipped onto its roof, collapsing the convertible top, shattering the windshield. The driver's door was ajar but jammed against a rock and he couldn't pull it open. The window was rolled down but the mangled roof made it impossible to see inside.

The slightest jarring could cause the car to shift position. Yet he had to risk it. He had to know if "she" was in there. He swung his spotlight around and pointed the beam on the torn rear window.

Colefield had looked inside wrecks before and braced himself. He had recovered bodies from lakes, fanning his hands around in zero visibility until he felt something stir in the murky silt. Seeing a phantom head floating around in dirty river water was enough to bring bile to his lips. He had pulled cadavers from rivers that had dragged along the bottom for months before finally surfacing — the stench of decay suffocating. He'd retrieved appendages chopped off by props, found beloved pets that had fallen or been thrown from boats. Last month it had been a child, an accidental drowning on the Sandy River. And, of course, far too many homicide victims, mangled, disfigured and dumped.

Over the years he had unearthed a private place to store the darkest memories and the stench of decay, because nothing prepares a person for absorbing death in all its forms. Nothing.

And it would make it that much more difficult tonight because he was sure this was Nicole's car.

He shined the beam of light through the opening.

"She" wasn't there. No one was.

4

The sun was just spreading its warming light over the snowcapped peak on Mt. Hood when the recovery team took a break. The Lieutenant told Colefield to take a time out. They'd done their job. The car was ashore. No bodies were found. They could resume their search later.

Weaver had already gone ashore with Bart and had stripped out of his gear and was toweling his hair dry along the riverbank.

Colefield walked toward them unzipping the top half of his wetsuit when someone shouted they'd spotted something.

In a patch of tall reeds, one of the pleasure craft had caught a glimpse of a possible body.

The deputies ran over to look.

It couldn't have been closer. Along a narrow portion of beach there stood a thick patch of cattails. It was 100 feet upstream so no one had searched it. Colefield was well ahead of Bart and Weaver as he approached where the boat owner was shining a portable spotlight into the grass from the cockpit of his Boston Whaler.

It was next to impossible to see anything lying in the thick willowy cattails — a miracle really that the boat owner had spotted it — just a bare foot sticking out of a soaked blue dress. Colefield stooped down and cleared the grass back from her face. Her wet dark hair was tangled in the reeds. Her body covered in glass shards, no shoes, no necklace, only a pair of dangly gold earrings.

Nicole...

He checked her vitals. The wrist felt cool but there was a faint pulse. He held her hand. The fingers were lifeless.

"Get the paramedics over here!"

Within a matter of moments, the deputies helped the paramedics carry the unconscious doctor up the steep embankment. She had a nasty contusion on her forehead and cuts on her face. The men loaded her into the ambulance. The paramedics told Colefield to step back but he hesitated.

He looked down at her blue evening dress. It had a small tear on the right shoulder, which he assumed happened during the crash.

"Deputy. We'll do our best."

The doors closed. The ambulance sped off, sirens wailing. Soon it was just a reddish mirage in the dawn light.

Weaver walked over to Colefield. "It's a miracle, eh?"

Weaver's long face was puffy and still red from the tight-fitting dive mask and the frigid water temperature. When Colefield didn't respond, he frowned.

"I know her." Colefield was distraught, feeling sick to his stomach. "We met yesterday at the moorage. She's my new neighbor."

Weaver just stared at him momentarily, gathering his thoughts. When he spoke, his words sounded awkward. "The consensus is it was an accident. Maybe she underestimated the curves or was texting. If you all had been drinking earlier then maybe she was impaired. It's late. She could have just dozed off behind the wheel. Hell, she could have swerved to miss a possum or raccoon crossing the road. Take your pick. At this stage, it's a damn guessing game until we get a statement."

As Colefield stood there staring off into space, Bart walked over and interrupted. "Lieutenant wants a word." He held out a handheld radio to Colefield.

"It's Colefield, sir."

"Take the guys back to the office. Go get yourself some sleep. We'll do a follow-up later."

He stared at Weaver. "Sir I'd like to make another sweep."

"You have reason to believe we missed something?"

"No, sir. But..."

A plane taking off nearby interfered with their conversation. "Not now, Colefield. Tell me later. Call it quits."

The Lieutenant signed off. Colefield sighed and handed the radio back to Bart.

"Load up the gear."

Weaver looked relieved.

While Bart and Weaver carried equipment down to the sled, Colefield climbed up toward the road where one of the officers first on the scene sat in his patrol car, sipping some steaming coffee from a thermos.

Officer Brown rolled down his window, saluted a hello with his coffee cup. "Need some caffeine? I've got plenty."

"Why not..."

The officer set his cup down on the dash, reached across to the passenger seat toward a package of Styrofoam cups. He poured out some steaming liquid and held the cup out to the deputy.

Colefield took a sip. "You run the plates yet?"

"Car is registered to a Nicole Dafoe; address 656 Stockton Street, San Francisco, California. We found a purse in the vehicle that matches this information. A California license issued to a Dr. Nicole Dafoe, same address. At this point we have to assume that she was the sole person in the car since nothing else has turned up."

"Are there any other addresses for her?"

He put down his coffee, picked up his notebook. "Just that one. DOB 09-17-81. No priors. Looks like it just wasn't her night."

"Or maybe it was…"

"I suppose critical beats being dead. We'll have a better idea of how this went down once the hospital runs her blood work and if she comes around long enough for us to take a statement. Too bad she had to go through that. Car's too old for an airbag. A damn miracle she made it out alive."

"Where was the purse?"

"Floorboard, passenger side."

"What about a cell?"

"Toasted."

"You check the trunk?"

"There was a suitcase with a few clothing items."

"Could you read the identification tag?"

"The ink smeared like goose shit. Nothing inside to ID the belongings. It's all women's clothing though."

Colefield just shook his head. "You find skid marks?"

"Skid marks are sketchy now. We'll take another look when the light's better."

Colefield nodded. "Anything else in the trunk?"

"Just the usual stuff; flares, jack, spare."

"Who reported the accident?"

"A security guard for the Port of Portland. We took his statement and then released him. He was patrolling the airfield at the time. He didn't see much — just glimpsed the car. By the time he crossed the runway and got here, it had sunk. Good thing he trusted his instincts and called us."

"Any other witnesses?"

"No one has come forward."

Colefield looked up. In the distance was the beacon of the airport tower and the surrounding airfield. It was a good half-mile or so away.

All he had to go on was an attractive woman who had showed up on Montgomery's deck yesterday afternoon. She shared a bit of her life, tossed back a little alcohol and showed skill at fishing. Inquiring about the services of a bodyguard had changed the tone of the conversation. Her asking about protection now took on new meaning. The accident stirred a dozen questions in his mind.

"You got the purse?"

"It's in the trunk."

The purse was in an evidence bag sitting upright along with some police gear. Colefield looked at the contents in the glow of the trunk's dome light. The wallet held a California license, a few credit cards, a few business cards, one from a realtor, another one from a hairdresser in the Pearl, and what looked like a key card from a hotel. He found an ID pass from the VA hospital in Portland with her name on it, which was recently issued.

He put the ID down and unfolded a soggy restaurant receipt stowed away beneath one of the credit cards but he could still make it out. The $36 bar tab was from Jill's place — the Sextant Bar and Galley on Marine Drive. The date and time of the receipt were from last night. It was about the last thing he ever expected to find.

He stuck the receipt in his pocket and closed the trunk lid.

Officer Brown had gone over to take a final look at the crumpled-up convertible. Colefield joined him.

"Find anything interesting in the purse?"

Colefield shook his head. He could still feel the smudged ink on his fingertips. "Call me later if anything turns up."

"Maybe she'll get another shot. You never know…"

Brown turned and gave the signal to the operator. The battered Mercedes chassis creaked skyward as it was hoisted up onto the flatbed, every cable groaning under duress.

Colefield stepped back as a wave of water gushed from the wreckage pooling around his feet. When it was clear, he moved in for a last look. Was the rear bumper damaged? He couldn't tell with all the sludge.

Brown yawned. "All I see is mud."

5

By 0830, Colefield was done writing up his report. Another shift would take over soon. The Coast Guard had been called in to get eyes from the sky and they were ready to call it quits. They radioed that they would make a final sweep before heading back to their base at Swan Island. No floater had turned up.

At this point, until they heard otherwise, everybody was assuming Nicole Dafoe had been the sole occupant. Until she was conscious, there would be no way to confirm this.

An hour later, Colefield drug his body down the Portland Rowing Club ramp. While he dug around for his keys he heard his landlord's door creak open.

Montgomery limped out onto the walkway in his tattered bathrobe to get the morning newspaper. The men nodded in passing.

"You look like shit, Deputy!"

"Looks are only half of it."

"You want me to debrief you?"

"Later, Bill. I need some sleep."

Montgomery frowned. "Sleep is over-rated. You'll figure that out when you're my age."

"For now, I'll take what I can get."

"Well, if you're up by happy hour, come by for a drink. I'll pull out another bottle of tequila in case our neighbor is out prancing about in her bikini."

Colefield almost broke down and spilled the news but that would lead to a very long drawn out story that could wait. "If anyone around here makes any noise, you have my permission to shoot them." Colefield walked off toward his front door. Montgomery hobbled right behind, two crippled up sailors working their way home.

By early afternoon, after a few hours of sleep, Colefield was feeling more human. There had been no updates about Nicole or her accident. He made some strong black coffee, briefly toying with the idea of adding a shot of Irish whisky to it. He carried the cup into the living room, sat down and turned on the radio to a jazz station. Coltrane was playing. It didn't fit his mood, so he dialed in an easy-rock station, got bored with that quickly and turned it off. Content now with silence, he headed to make breakfast.

When he opened the refrigerator door, the strong odor of fish wafted out. Slabs of stacked pink meat brought on a flood of memories and blew any hope of a pleasant mood out the window.

He tossed the fish into the sink and reached over to turn on the garbage disposal when something caught his eye outside the kitchen window. Calico Jack paced back and forth along the sill. Colefield snatched the fish back onto the counter.

He walked over and opened the window holding a slab of pink meat. "There's more where that came from, buddy." After a moment's hesitation, Jack gobbled it up.

Colefield had to force down his own meal. Out of ham, he threw together an omelet made with Tillamook cheese, sautéed onions, and a can of Hormel's chili. He shook on some Tabasco sauce for some kick, and chased it all down with a glass of almond milk very near expiration.

With food in his belly, his mood improved. He took a hot shower, pulled on some shorts, a Bengal Tigers T-shirt, a pair of flip-flops and headed out the door.

He took a quick walk around Nicole's place and didn't see anything out of the ordinary. The windows were locked as were the front and back doors.

He wrapped loudly on his landlord's door and pushed it open.

"Who goes there?" A loud voice boomed from inside.

"It's me, Bill!"

"Colefield, old boy, good to see you. I'm nearly out of hooch."

"Sorry to disappoint you, but I don't have any booze with me. I'll go to the liquor store later."

Colefield closed the door and entered the galley. Montgomery came hobbling down the stairs in khaki pants, a faded NRA T-shirt, and crusty tennis shoes so old his big toes had worn holes through the tops. He was packing an ammo box.

"Give me a hand with this, would you?"

Colefield took the heavy box from him and set it down on the floor by the stairs.

"What'd you have in there? 50-caliber?"

"Special rounds for a fellow vet coming by later. All handmade. I call them limp dicks. They have enough powder to spin them out of the muzzle and travel about twenty yards with nice velocity then they peter out. Navy Seals used them once upon a time, so did the Green Berets and a few other elite teams. I got the recipe from an old friend…"

"What are they used for?"

"Close quarter killing. Keeps collateral damage to a minimum."

"Contract work?"

"You know I don't pry into my client's enterprises. They bring me their requests. I do the job. Once my work is done, I wash my hands of it. I sleep better at night."

"You want me to do background checks on all these characters? You're talking to a deputy who has a right to be worried."

"Don't be worried about this one. He's a pro."

"That's what I'm afraid of."

Montgomery sat in front of a telescope on a tripod pointed toward the river.

"I need a favor," Colefield said. "I need to get inside our neighbor's houseboat."

"That's a devilish good idea. Why not try knocking on her door?"

"She's in the hospital."

"Good god that's inconvenient. Did the tequila do her in?"

"Possibly."

"She came by last night looking for you. I tried to wile her away. She was having none of it."

"When?"

"Just after a double Pusser's and a picturesque sunset."

"Why didn't you bang on my door?"

"Why would I want to do that? We were having a rather grand time of our own."

"What did she want?"

"Wanted to know where you were? She tried the tender, you weren't there. She thought you might be here, guzzling down my booze."

"I was helping Bernie with a boat problem."

Montgomery scratched his shaggy beard. "She wanted to hire you. I told her you could be 'had'. All it would require would be a stack of greenbacks that I would be more than happy to hold onto as a deposit on next month's rent."

"Hire me for what?"

"Rough somebody up."

"She said that?"

"Not in so many words..." Montgomery dry coughed. "Some of the old juice came back flirting with her. She's a keeper, old boy. What happened?"

"A car accident."

Montgomery pushed the telescope aside and slowly climbed to his feet. He grabbed his cane hanging over the back of a chair and hobbled over to the kitchen sink and spat out what looked like chewing tobacco.

"Will the woman be all right?"

"I don't know. So, what else did she discuss with you?"

Montgomery swiped his bare arm over his crusty chapped lips. "A pair of beauties showed up and whisked her away before I had time to interrogate her further. It doesn't take much to distract a horny old bastard like me. If it makes you feel any better, she didn't want to talk in front of her friends." Montgomery pulled a handkerchief from his back pocket. "Do you think it was an accident or something more sinister?"

"Nobody knows anything yet."

"I should have tied her up," Montgomery said.

"Grab your lock pick set and follow me next door."

6

Colefield figured Nicole's rear door seemed like the best point of entry. What exactly he thought he'd find in the houseboat wasn't at the forefront. The more urgent issue was not getting busted by a stranger while breaking in.

A small boat idled by out of the moorage, its gurgling 2-stroke engine spitting out little puffs of blue smoke into an otherwise clear sky. Colefield kept an eye on the driver, who seemed intently focused on the channel markers beneath the Sellwood Bridge — too busy steering to take notice of their dubious activities.

After the boat was out of sight, Montgomery pulled out what looked like a jackknife. There were other gadgets bulging from his pockets as backup devices.

"What is that thing?"

"It's the latest and greatest, old boy. A JPXS-6. Got it online. Has six fancy pick devices that work on the most common locks. American Locks take plenty of practice. Now Master Locks are a breeze. Mortise Locks, on the other hand … well, let's just say you need a little extra patience, which you, my boy, are in short supply of. You want to give it a try?"

"No."

"I rest my case."

"Can we do this before the police arrive?"

"Don't get your girdle in a knot." Montgomery looked down at the French door lock. He eyed it carefully, and then looked the door frame up and down. "Piece of cake," he said.

"It's a little newer than I prefer, but that will work to our advantage. What we have here is a Schlage Camelot Single Cylinder. Basic stuff. I have a similar style on my front door, but I went with solid brass. I had the tumblers custom made, built like Sherman tanks. I was hoping for something a little more challenging. They could have made it tougher on us by using a three-point locking system but I can get by those, too. Living here all these years has given me plenty of time to perfect my expertise with locks and my talents at getting damsels in distress or drunken sailors back inside their abodes. Can't tell you how many keys have fallen into the drink, or bikinis, for that matter. They both require immediate attention, although the latter is less urgent. Hell, look at this door. The wood is just a cunt hair over an inch thick and the glass is so thin we practically could cut it with a butter knife. Now if you look at my place. I've got hurricane glass thick enough to deflect a missile."

"Just open the lock, please."

Montgomery selected a wiggly shaped three-inch blade with points in various configurations and stuck it into the lock. He gently shook and lifted and twisted the device in and out until the tumblers lined up and the lock sprang open. Just that fast…

"Presto!" he crowed, looking a bit surprised by his own accomplishment.

"Nice job."

"I have to confess something."

"Can it wait until we're inside?"

"Good point, old boy. I almost forgot we're on a mission. Why are we doing this again?"

Montgomery put his jackknife back into his pocket while Colefield turned the knob. Both men stepped inside. Colefield quickly scanned the walls looking for a main alarm box. He didn't see one.

"There's no alarm," Montgomery said.

"How do you know that?"

"I've been here before."

"You were schtupping Maddie?"

"My lips are sealed."

The houseboat was larger than Colefield's bachelor pad but not by much. The interior walls were white stucco with built-in alcoves and benches with dark hardwood trim. There was no furniture to speak of, no tables, chairs, lamps, bookcases. It was bare-bones as Nicole had implied. The kitchen was fair sized with cast iron hooks hanging down from the ceiling for pots and pans. The tile counter had a couple empty champagne bottles and plastic cups sitting around, a few gifts, some wrapping paper strewn about, along with an ice chest resting on the tile floor. It had a few bottles of imported beer floating in mostly melted ice.

The familiar bottle of tequila sat next to the cooler. It was about two-thirds full, which gave Colefield some relief. There was a gas stove and a stainless refrigerator in the corner. He opened the frig, and the only thing in it was a partially eaten piece of white cake with pink icing. Behind him, stucco shelving and two hardwood cabinets were as bare as the rest of the place. In what would have been the master bedroom, there were a few clothes hanging up: two tops, fresh out of the package, a clean white blouse, a pair of tan slacks, and a black bathing suit. On the floor were a pair of sensible heels and a pair of stylish sandals Nicole had worn the previous day.

Colefield remembered her long tanned legs, the slender curve of her hips, her crooked beautiful smile, and hazel eyes that sparkled with life. The woman he had seen lying on the gurney in the back of the ambulance did not resemble that memory. He hoped one day soon, she would.

Montgomery hobbled into the room carrying a few items in his hand. "She didn't plan on bunking here last night."

"I agree with you. They found a suitcase in her car with a few changes of clothes. She's probably living in a hotel or with some friends."

"Well this gives sparseness new meaning."

"Is there a front closet?"

"Roger that. There's a jacket in there."

"Did you find anything?"

Montgomery held up two paperbacks. The covers were shiny and new. Colefield read both titles: *How to Date Men* and *Cooking in the Nude for Women.*

"These were on a shelf. Interesting photographs in the second one," Montgomery said. "Care to look?"

Colefield reached out and took the first book. He thumbed the pages until he found a half-dozen or more greeting cards. He pulled them out and passed the book back to Montgomery. The salutations were short and sweet, the handwriting neat and tidy, the sentences contrite — nothing exceptional or personable. A few were signed, first names only. The one from Grace had been purchased at the airport.

"Bill, hand me the other book."

When he opened the second, it contained a small photograph tucked inside the jacket that dropped onto the floor. He stooped over and picked it up. The color photograph was of a 30ish-looking man with an athletic build and dark hair. The man wore tennis shorts and a pink polo shirt. A heavy gold chain hung around his neck and a large gold watch dangled from his left wrist. In the opposite hand, he held a tennis racket down at his side and he was smiling into the lens as the picture was taken. The background was blurred but it looked like it was shot in the tropics. There were palm fronds and sand at the fringe of the image.

Colefield took another good long look. The background gave no clue really — could have been at a resort or most any tropical place. Definitely, though, there was a family resemblance between the man in the photo and image he had of Nicole: the almond shaped chin, the lean and long athletic body type, the same long fingers, the same skin tone, and the same large eyes. He checked the back of the photo. It was blank.

Colefield handed the photograph to Montgomery for his opinion. Montgomery pulled out his cheaters, looked at the picture grinding his gums as if it made him uncomfortable.

"A pinko faggot," he said, and dropped it into Colefield's hand.

"What exactly does that mean?"

"Guy looks like a pussy. He's got the gaudy gold chain and Rolex and ball hugging shorts to prove it. And only queers play tennis."

Colefield pulled out his cell phone and took snapshots of the photograph in case he needed to refer to it later. "Did you discover anything else in the house?"

"She's as bare as an empty piggy bank."

Colefield started toward the door. "You coming?" he said.

Montgomery removed his cheaters and put them inside his shirt pocket. He hesitated, staring across the room. "In a manner of speaking," he said with some tenderness. "Madeline's bed was in the center of the room by the window," he pointed it out. "One of those waterbeds hippies had in the seventies. It was all slosh and wiggles and giggles with her. She was a fun old broad." Montgomery swiped a sentimental tear. "Stay single, my boy. Women are nothing but trouble…" Montgomery spotted a black bikini hanging in the closet. He walked over, removed it from the hanger, tucked it into his pocket and hobbled out of the room.

As the old pirate had said, there was a tailored jacket hanging up in the front closet. Colefield checked the pockets. There was a wadded-up Kleenex in the left side, a pen in the breast pocket, and nothing in the right side.

He caught up with his partner in crime in the kitchen, screwing the lid back on the bottle of tequila. The bottle of wine and gifts were still on the counter undisturbed.

"No use letting this go to waste," Montgomery said, and walked off toward the back door carrying the jug of booze.

Outside Nicole's houseboat, the sun seemed harsher and the air now had a more pungent smell. The wind had shifted. A brownish cloud of noxious gas from a bottleneck on the I-5 freeway hovered over the river. Colefield figured the whole world was going to hell — a defeatist attitude and one he didn't appreciate in others. He locked the door and followed Montgomery back to his place.

Montgomery reached into his rear pocket and pulled out a small black book. He handed it to Colefield. "You might want to look at this."

"Where'd you get that?"

"From the jacket in the closet."

Colefield thumbed through the small notebook filled with pages of indecipherable scribbling.

"It's shorthand," Montgomery offered.

"OK. Can you read any of it?"

"I'll translate it using my old texts and give you a full report by tomorrow."

"Anything else you're withholding?"

"You just focus on the man in the photograph. He may be next of kin, because you don't go around packing just one photograph. I'll do my magic on this little ledger. We can return it before she gets out of the hospital. And she'll never be the wiser."

Colefield handed it over.

"Did you see anyone hanging around her place last night?"

"I was half to the wind by sunset, old boy. My snooping skills, I admit, have fallen by the wayside."

"Can you check with the other neighbors?"

"Yes. But first, your fellow brother-in-arms needs his daily dose of medication. Care to join me?"

7

After Colefield checked in with the office by phone, he hurried to Legacy Emanuel Hospital. Yes, they had admitted Doctor Nicole Dafoe. She was in the trauma unit, Room 421. He was told he could take the elevators at the end of the corridor.

He got off on the fourth floor, bumping into an exhausted male nurse carrying a heavy load of files, deep creases biting at his brow. The man clutched the items to his chest much the same way a priest would hold a cherished Bible. Colefield stopped the door with his foot. He pulled out his credentials.

"What do you want, deputy? I'm terribly busy."

"What can you tell me about the patient in room 421? Her name is Nicole Dafoe."

"You'll need to speak with her doctor."

"And who would that be?"

"Dr. Phillip. But she isn't here."

"Have any next of kin been notified about her condition?"

The nurse seemed preoccupied and in a hurry. Colefield glanced at the name tag pinned to his scrubs. "Blake, it's important or I wouldn't ask."

Blake let out a pained sigh. "I'd have to check her file."

The walk to the nursing station seemed endless. They eventually stopped at a counter and Blake dumped the files, ensconced himself behind a computer and punched information into a worn keyboard. The screen came to life.

"It's Doctor Nicole Dafoe," Colefield reminded him, assuming the trauma unit was like most hospital emergency rooms, lots of people coming and going, lots of faces and names jumbled together.

"Yes, yes, I know. It indicates her next of kin have not been notified."

"Why?"

"I presume Admitting doesn't know who they are. Besides, isn't that your job?"

Colefield bit his tongue. "Has her blood work come back?"

"Yes."

"Any signs of alcohol or drugs in her system?"

Blake stared at him and wasn't giving in.

"Look, you're right. I should speak with her doctor. What's her contact information?"

"She'll be back on duty at 11pm. You can call this desk. If the doctor is available, they'll put you through or take your information down at that time."

"What's the number?"

The nurse read it off. Colefield entered it into his cell. He needed to know what the toxicology report indicated. He wouldn't be able to think clearly until he did. "Blake, I may appear to be just another cop digging for information. But Ms. Dafoe is my neighbor. I'm very concerned."

The nurse looked him in the eye and wasn't totally sold on the story but he was smart enough to know the rather large deputy wasn't going anywhere until he had what he wanted.

The nurse scrolled through the file. "Her BAC was .06 percent, below the legal limit. No drugs were noted in the report."

The nurse continued. "Ms. Dafoe's condition is unstable. She suffered a severe contusion, some internal bleeding, and a mild case of hypothermia. You can call this evening after the doctor has had a chance to make her rounds; she may be able to give you an update then."

"Thank you for your time, Blake." Colefield turned and glanced down the busy corridor. Nurses and doctors charged by, complicated life-support equipment and monitors were being wheeled down toward room 421. At the last minute, they turned and entered the room across from Nicole's. A uniformed officer sat in a folding chair outside that room and jumped up when the medical personnel rushed inside.

"The elevators are behind you, deputy."

"Why is there a guard watching one of the rooms?"

"A few nights ago, an administrator at the VA was assaulted. She's under police protection. She's in critical condition."

"Where did it happen?"

"In the parking lot..."

"I didn't hear anything about it."

"They're withholding the story. The police think somebody might try and finish the job if they know she's alive. That's why she was admitted under a Jane Doe."

"Do you know who's in charge of the investigation?"

"I wouldn't have the slightest idea."

The telephone rang at the desk. The nurse picked it up and spoke in a very calm and professional manner. He hung up, jumped up from the desk and scurried off down the hall in the direction of the chaos. Colefield followed behind.

When he got close to the room, the guard stepped forward and put up his hand. Colefield pulled out his credentials. "What's going on in there?"

"I guess she stopped breathing."

"I heard she was assaulted. Any suspects yet?"

The man frowned. "What's your business here?"

"I've got a neighbor in the room across the hall."

"I was here when they brought her in."

"Who's in charge of investigating the assault on the administrator?"

"They brought in some Fed."

"Any suspects?"

"Zip."

"Pretty strange that both these women work for the VA…"

"I heard your neighbor was in an automobile accident."

"That's what we're investigating."

Colefield glanced over the guard's shoulder. He could see two nurses and one doctor in the room working frantically to keep the woman alive. The male nurse was assisting and would be tied up for a while, which would give him all the time he needed.

"Take care, officer…"

He crossed the hall and went inside room 421. Nicole sat partially upright in bed with all sorts of electrical leads and hoses and IV lines attached to her chest and arms. Her eyes were closed. An oxygen mask was strapped to her mouth. A TV mounted on the wall was turned on, the volume down low. He'd been around a few people in induced comas and there never seemed to be much going on mentally and Nicole was no exception. Her face was drawn, bruised, and lifeless. She appeared to be breathing; her chest rising and falling very slowly, her vitals lit up on the machine indicating a blood pressure of 112 over 75, pulse 66, body temp of 99.9. There were no flowers or cards in the room, no magazines, and no personal items whatsoever. It was bleak and sterile. It would be a horrible place to die. He couldn't bear that thought. He stood at the bottom of the bed and reached down and stoked her leg to reassure her she was not alone. After there was no reaction to his touch, he stepped into the hallway and closed the door. The staff across the hall filed out of the room looking forlorn and whispering.

Blake stopped and spoke with the guard. He looked over, spotted Colefield and walked over, frowning.

"You don't give up, do you deputy?"

"How's the administrator?"

"Only about fifty percent make it," he said without emotion. "She wasn't one of them."

In the parking lot, Colefield sat in his old truck clutching his Blackberry, staring down at the screen. He was thinking about the VA Administrator who had just died. There were no family members standing by, no friends. The same as his neighbor in the room across the hall and it left him feeling raw inside.

He searched his Blackberry again and could find nothing on the administrator. Something didn't feel right.

Colefield punched up the digital version of the Oregonian and scanned the headlines for something on Nicole's accident and found a brief police notice, short and to the point. No personal information about Nicole had been given out.

He called his bud Harvey Feinstein with homicide division and asked if he'd tap into his database to see if he could track down anything on Nicole. Then he asked about the assault on the administrator from the VA. Harvey couldn't talk about it.

Frustrated by no next of kin, and a no-name photo, Colefield decided it was time to go in a different direction.

8

The Sextant tavern had thinned out. The parking lot had only a few stragglers. The deputies cut across the damp grass to the front porch and went inside.

It'd been weeks since he'd found the courage to face Jill again. He tried but things had gone south immediately. She was seeing someone else now and wanted nothing to do with him. He hadn't given up completely, popping in from time to time, after work, to unwind and see if things had changed. Jill's new boyfriend was an asshole in his opinion. Whatever she saw in the tight-assed bastard, Colefield could only surmise. Having more money than God may have played a part or maybe he had a very large pecker, which was not the image Colefield wanted to carry around with him every time he saw the guy smirking at him across the bar.

But tonight, the rich bastard wasn't there. And Jill, who looked up as he approached the empty bar stool next to his co-workers, actually gave him a hint of a smile, seemed happy to see him — almost.

"Look who the cat drug in," she said as he flopped down beside Weaver.

"How ya been, Jill?"

"Peachy. You?"

"Working a lot."

"That's what the boys say. What do you want to drink?"

"Coffee."

"Pots dry. Pick something else."

"The IPA is pretty good," Bart said, slurping the foamy head off his fresh pint.

"It's too hoppy for me," Weaver said. "Here — you try it."

He slid the glass over in front of Colefield. "Jill," Weaver said. "If Mr. Charming wants the beer, please pour me something less green."

Colefield slid the beer aside. "Get him what he wants. I'll take water. And put them on my tab."

Jill smirked and walked off to pour Weaver a new pint. A busty waitress slapped Bart's shoulder, happy to see him. "Hey Barty, where ya been?"

Hearing the waitress' playful banter, Bart blushed. It was clear he had a secret admirer.

"Ah, I've been pulling some overtime last few weeks."

"Well, I'm still up for what we talked about. I've got the next two days off. What's your schedule like?"

Weaver butted in. "You've got the next two days off — right, Bart?" he turned and winked at Colefield.

The waitress wrote down her number on the back of a napkin and slapped it down on the bar in front of Bart. "Call me. It'll be fun. We'll go see *Incredible III*. Then we'll see how incredible you can be."

She winked at the deputy, scooped her drink order, and sauntered off, happy as a clam. Weaver and Colefield smiled at each other while Jill dropped a fresh beer down in front of Weaver and a glass of water in front of him.

"I've got to talk to you about something," Colefield said, and slugged back a gulp of water.

"In case you're wondering … he turned out to be a freak. A little crooked dick — just as you said."

With that, Jill marched off and dealt with a few customers at the end of the bar. Colefield hadn't expected that confession. The news was both encouraging and unsettling. He certainly cared for Jill — probably even loved her, but it'd been a rocky road and he'd let her down several times. Even if he did want to rekindle the relationship, it would take some finessing. And at the moment, he didn't know how much finessing he had left in him

"Wow — that was an earful," Weaver leaned over and said. "You going back to the shed tonight?"

"Yeah … I've been meaning to ask you — did you hear anything about a VA Administrator getting assaulted?"

Weaver frowned, rubbing his bushy eyebrows. "No. Why?"

"I don't know. It's probably nothing."

"Trust your gut, that's what you always say to Bart."

"When I was at the hospital today checking on Ms. Dafoe there was an officer guarding one of the patients across the hall. I figured the DA was probably being cautious so they threw a uniform on her door. But I didn't get the whole story. She died while I was there. Everyone was pretty tight-lipped."

"VA is taking a lot of heat right now…"

"It could have been some ex-boyfriend or ex-husband who went off the deep end, or some whacko nut job who wanted to make a point. Whatever, it got my attention. And if it's some crazy ass vet who just got fed up with the system, it could mean a trend."

"You ask Bart about it?"

"He said there's nothing on any of the social media sites."

Colefield looked over and stole a look at Jill at the end of the bar. She smiled back with a twisted little cute-ass twinkle in her eye.

Colefield pulled out a wad of singles and tossed them down. "Bart, go plug something into the jukebox. This place needs some atmosphere."

Bart polished off his beer, signaled to Jill for a refill, and left.

Weaver slurped down a big gulp of beer leaving a foamy thin line along his mustache. He swiped his lip and slid his glass aside. "Got time for a game of pool?"

"Hit Bart up. Jill and I need to talk."

"Your funeral..."

Weaver burped and got up off his stool, headed toward the pool tables across the room. Jill closed out a tab with one of the customers, poured a beer for Bart and sent it off with the busty waitress to deliver. She wiped her hands on a bar towel and fussed with her hair. She had on a snug black sleeveless Nike shirt and faded blue jeans that followed the curve of her thighs. A flashy bandana was tied around her neck for added affect. She moved toward him, cowboy boots clicking across the floor like the final countdown of a time clock. He couldn't have pried his eyes away from her for a million bucks.

Planting her elbows on the bar, she leaned in, lips glistening and very inviting. "You said you had something you wanted to talk about?"

"I've missed you, Jill."

Her face softened but she was no fool. She kept her guard up. Colefield leaned in a little closer, testing the water. She held her ground.

"Easy does it, cowboy. One day at a time, OK?"

"Fair enough." Colefield paused. "I don't know if you heard all the commotion on Marine Drive last night, but I need to ask you a few questions about an accident."

"That's why you came in?" Jill shot him a disgusted look.

The mood was gone.

"A Mercedes went off the road about a mile from here..."

Jill interrupted. "Yeah, yeah, I heard all about it. Someone from County stopped in for some coffee afterward, told me all the gory details. And we're revisiting this why?"

"The driver stopped in here that night. He dug into his pocket, pulled out the receipt he had taken from Nicole's purse, dropped it on the bar. Any idea who served her?"

Jill glanced down at the receipt. The implication was written all over her face. "Great. Looks like I did. Got a description?"

He did his best to tell her.

She listened and then stepped back, shaking her head in disbelief. "You're shitting me?" she said with spite in her voice. "So — you're the guy? Well, she kept drooling over this handsome deputy she met that afternoon to her friend. Of course, how would I know? I didn't put two and two together, until now. It's you, isn't it?"

"Someone was with her?"

"Yeah, sure. Another chick."

"What'd she look like?"

"Regal and courtly. Didn't engage with me much. I can't believe it. And to think I actually felt happy to see you tonight. How did she put it to her friend: 'He's so witty ... so strong...' You sure won her over, Jason. Just so your ego gets knocked down a notch or two — you did zip on the impressive scale for the friend. Well, if this just isn't another chapter in Jill and Jason's little book of horror. What are the fuckin' odds?"

"Jill, settle down."

She started to walk off. He reached out and grabbed her wrist. "Jill — I swear — I didn't instigate anything. I was fishing. She came over with a beer and introduced herself. Nothing more."

"It always starts with fishing. Then you add beer into the mixture and before you know it — you're flopping around on a nice cozy bed."

"Look, this is awkward but we really need to discuss a few things. It's for your own protection. I'm not the bad guy here. So, you served them? What else?"

"Give me a minute," she said, and took a few deep breaths. "Ok. I can do this. What do you need from me, shithead?"

"Were they alone?"

"Yes."

"Were they sober when they left?"

"Of course — I run a respectable business. I'd like to keep it that way and not get sued. You just dropped a bomb at my doorstep. Now I'm going to have to answer an OLCC inquiry, deal with your cop buddies. Then they'll be the insurance investigators and lawyers that will come knocking. See if they can pin her accident on me for over-serving."

She sagged back against the bar and stared off in space. He felt like a heel but life sometimes dished out unfairness in unequal portions. She seemed to snap out it and focused her attention back on him.

She moved closer, staring back with wet emerald eyes. "Her friend was tipsy but she wasn't driving. Look, this lady wasn't drunk. I gathered her friend was from out of town. Here for a housewarming or something. Anyway, they had an appetizer and a few drinks. They were killing time. Your girlfriend was planning on taking her to the airport. Her friend was catching a red-eye back to New York."

"Did you see anyone else around that night? Anyone follow them out?"

"No and no."

"The driver is lying in Emanuel in a trauma unit in a coma. We don't know if there was a passenger or not. The time on the receipt and the time of the accident are about an hour apart. That's good news. Maybe she dropped her friend at the airport and was on her way back when the accident happened."

Jill buried her face in her hands.

"I'm going to interview a guy at the airport tonight who called it in. Maybe he can give some clarity on what happened."

Jill gathered herself together.

"Look, her friend's name was Grace," he said. "I don't know her last name. If I had it, I could make an inquiry with the airlines..."

"Her last name is Jones. Grace Jones. She offered to pay the tab but her card was declined. I read the name before I handed it back."

"Grace Jones, perfect." Colefield jotted it down on a napkin.

"Jesus, Jason — if I lose this place what will I do? I bitch about it. I'm stressed out most of the time. I'm accountable for fifteen wait staff, four cooks, three bartenders, an accountant, and a bookkeeper. But do I want to be unemployed? I don't think so. Of course, if I lost this place, then maybe I could move to Panama. Forget about things like a boyfriend standing you up for a romantic weekend while he sleeps with his ex." Jill folded her arms across her chest. "So, is there anything else?"

"Her bloodwork came back. She was under the legal limit."

Jill's shoulders relaxed as she took a deep breath. Jason resisted the urge to reach across the bar and touch her. She seemed lost in thought. "I got the impression she was upset about something. Perhaps just that she didn't seem to want to see her friend go."

"Did Grace have a purse with her?"

"Not a purse, a large wallet, black with gold trim, nothing flashy. She took the credit card out of it and touched up her makeup before they left."

"We didn't find a second purse at the scene."

"If this accident hadn't happened, would you still have come in here tonight?"

* * *

Before Colefield left the bar, he made a call to the airlines. Ms. Jones had flown out the previous night on Delta Flight 1240 to New York. That was good news. At least he could check her off the dead passenger list.

Wanting privacy, he waited to make a second call from work.

He recognized her smug voice immediately. "Yes, this is Ms. Jones, who's calling please? It's very late."

"It's Deputy Colefield, ma'am. I'm Nicole's neighbor. We met briefly at the moorage…"

"What can I do for you?"

"I'm afraid I have some bad news. Nicole was involved in an accident last night."

"God — is she OK?"

"She's recovering in the hospital. We believe it happened after she dropped you off at the airport."

Colefield filled her in giving her a moment to process it.

"She was fine when she left. I was a mess but Nicole is tough. She can handle separations better than me. We've been friends since college."

"Did you notice if anyone was following her after she left the airport?"

"She dropped me at curbside. It was pretty busy, so there were cars. But I didn't see anything suspicious."

"We're having difficulty tracking down her next of kin. Can you help us out?"

"Have you contacted Jesse?" she asked.

"Who's that?"

"Her sibling. They've been close since childhood. I haven't seen him in years but I think he's living in San Francisco now."

"Can you give me Jesse's information?"

"Let me see if I have it written down somewhere. One moment, deputy," she said and put the telephone down. When she came back on the line she rattled it off.

"One last thing? Did Nicole mention anything about wanting to hire a bodyguard?"

"What on earth for?"

"Then I take it the bodyguard wasn't for you?"

"I'm going through a divorce. But I certainly don't need protection. You're starting to frighten me, deputy. I thought you said this was an accident."

"We're still looking into the matter. Was there anyone else that was at the party who might have needed to hire a bodyguard?"

"I can't help you there. You'd have to contact them yourself. I can give you their information in an email later if that would be helpful."

He said it was and read off his email and cell phone. "Well, if you think of anything else, you have my number."

She disconnected.

He looked down at the number she had given him for Nicole's sibling and dialed it. At least the number went through. Unfortunately, it went through to an automated voice mail. He left a detailed message and told Jesse to contact him ASAP. He immediately received a response by text. It was short and to the point. Jesse was flying up from California as soon as possible and would be prepared to stay for however much time his sister needed. Perhaps they could meet at the hospital to discuss the details of the accident? Colefield texted back and told Jesse to contact him when he got in town.

9

Colefield parked near the runway gate, turned off his headlights and crawled out of the cruiser. A few minutes later, a dark blue pickup with a Port Authority emblem on the door pulled up. A man climbed out from behind the wheel, walked over to the gate and stuck his key into the lock and pushed it open.

"Thanks for meeting me," Colefield said. The man had on a dark blue uniform with a side arm attached to his hip. He grabbed Colefield's hand and gave it a firm shake. His weathered face looked to be a few years past retirement.

"I'm Fred Peterson. You got here pretty fast."

"I called you from the office five minutes from here."

The man turned and pointed in the opposite direction toward the airport. "Well, way down that road about 500 yards or so is where I saw most of it from."

Colefield noticed a dirt road that ran the length of the runway. The surrounding area was flat and the grass tall around the perimeter. A fence ran along Marine Drive to keep out intruders.

"Yeah, where we're standing now is probably as good as where I was at the time. It wasn't quite midnight, happened around 11:30. I didn't see much. Just saw some headlights, heard a pretty loud crash on the river. That was about it. I drove up to this gate. It was locked, which is what took me so long. The lock was rusty. My key almost snapped off before I finally got it opened and drove over to take a better look."

"Why don't you start with what you saw from the field?"

"Well, I saw headlights coming down Marine Drive at a pretty good clip. The second set trailed behind by half a mile or so at first —"

Colefield cut him off. "Second set? You mean there was more than one vehicle that night?"

"The other car was a long way back. I didn't pay much attention to it at first."

"Go on…"

"Both cars seemed to pick up speed. I didn't think anything of it, really. I see plenty of folks drive down Marine Drive all times of the night. Fifty percent of 'em clip right along. It's a long stretch of road, kind of curvy in spots, makes for an interesting drive if you've been drinking. Nothing seemed out of the ordinary at first."

"You're certain you saw two sets of headlights?"

"Yeah. That's where it kind of gets fuzzy … like I said the second set of lights were farther back. Then, they weren't."

"So, you're saying the second car caught up to the Mercedes?"

"Yeah."

"Did they try to pass?"

"I thought that's what they were going to do but they just came up on the other car and tailgated it. Then, I heard a noise and the car was gone. I couldn't tell if the second car even slowed down. Strange now that I think about it. Who wouldn't stop if they saw an accident happen in front of them?"

"It could have been a hit and run. Why didn't you mention this to the officer the night of the accident?"

"It happened so darn fast. I wasn't certain I saw what I did. I got some issues with my depth perception. At least I phoned it in though. I did that much."

"Were you able to make out the make or model of the second car?"

"I was too busy trying to get over there to see if I'd really seen what I thought or not. By then the second car was long gone."

"Was there anyone else around that night?"

The man thought it over. "It may have nothing to do with it. But there's this guy we call the River Rat. He prowls around at night. I've seen him all around this area. He might be homeless. He might live on a boat. I've never seen him with a vehicle. He always dresses in camo and carries a rifle and a tactical knife. We've been keeping an eye on him for months now. It all started when one of the other guards spotted the guy one night trespassing on Port property. Before he could confront him, the guy disappeared. I was just coming on shift and I let my supervisor know about it immediately. He took it up the chain of command. News came back that we were to allow him access to Port property. Turns out he is providing a valuable service, free-of-charge. He hunts birds. As you can imagine, they're a real problem for us. All birds in general, really. They fly into the path of planes when they take off or come in to land. They've busted windshields, fouled engines, even got tangled up in landing gear. We set off charges all the time to scare them away. A few years back the Port even contracted with a few specialized hunters to kill 'em. All that worked for a few weeks and then they came right back."

"Is he one of the hired hunters now?"

"No. As I said, I think he might live on the river. He comes ashore to hunt late at night. No one has ever gotten close enough to him to have a conversation."

"I'm surprised we haven't heard about him. Especially if he's running around shooting at birds."

"He doesn't do it for sport. He eats them. I've seen spots where he's gutted them out, left the feathers behind but never the head. The chief of security for the Port is a commander in the National Guard. He looked into the guy's background. He managed to get a few headshots with an infrared camera and they ran them through the DOD and Interpol's databases courtesy of Homeland Security. Turns out this guy had prior military training and a clean record. Once they figured out he wasn't some terrorist, they relaxed."

"What else did the DOD report indicate?"

"I can probably get you a copy if you're interested."

"Do that." Colefield took out a business card with his contact information and handed it to the guard.

"I know it sounds farfetched," the guard said. "Yet, we've got bean counters to prove it. They tally up the bird counts, what's migrating through, how many are in the area — all that stuff. Since this guy has been around, the goose population has dropped significantly. I think the birds are hip to him. They fear him now."

"What does he look like?"

"Never saw him up close, just from a distance."

"Didn't you say your head of security had photos?"

"I didn't see those images. But he's average height, quick on his feet, healthy overall. He can run up and down those embankments like Superman. I don't know if he's a rock climber or a magician. Maybe a little of both..."

"Why bring him up now?"

"It's just that I saw him that night. Before the accident. He's got this spot where he likes to dig under the fencing about an eighth-of-a-mile east of here. He usually covers the hole up after he's done his business. That night he didn't. Kind of odd. He's a very methodical character. I suspect he doesn't do one thing without knowing his next move in advance. I've known characters like him when I was in the service. My guess — he was in some kind of Special Ops unit."

"Did the report confirm this?"

"That's the thing ... there's some mystery behind his file. You'll see what I mean when you read it."

Colefield chewed on that for a moment. "You're saying he was around the crash site at the time of the accident?"

"I'm sure he was — but ghosts are easier to see."

10

The following morning, Colefield woke up with a headache, stiff neck, and an annoying ringing in his ears. His wild nightmares had left him wrecked. They ran the gamut of ghosts with chains holding Nicole underwater to him trying to provide cover for an unknown soldier with a squirming Calico Jack in his bloody hands. Crazy disturbing shit.

He crawled off the couch still in his clothes from the night before, ran a hand through his greasy hair, and tried to focus in on an empty whiskey bottle turned over on the end table. He uprighted it, clicked off the XM Radio that was playing loud country music — a different channel than he normally listened to. He couldn't remember much. He picked up the Sports Illustrated off the floor and tossed it onto the stack by the sofa and headed toward the kitchen. It didn't take a detective to figure out the situation. He must have passed out after polishing off the Bushmills.

Out in the kitchen he heard something outside the small window. Calico Jack jumped up on the sill and startled him. Shit — had he remembered to feed the damn cat?

Even if most nights, the straggler slept outside under the stars, prowling the marina for shrews or mice or the occasional stray pussy, they were more alike than not. Both loners, both hunters, with no one to answer to but each other.

He splashed some cold water on his face, dried it off with a paper towel and then wedged open the window so the cat could come inside.

The monster darted through the opening and jumped down on the counter looking frazzled and in worse shape than him. The cat's head was all slimy. A patch of fur was missing near his hind end. Splotches of what looked like blood or oil or something on his front legs.

"What the hell happened to us last night?" he mumbled to the cat. "C'mere. Let me take a look at you."

He corralled the animal and used a soapy washcloth to wipe off the slime plastering down the fur on the cat's head. It was lubricant, possibly from one of the outboard motors or transmission cables from one of the boats at the marina. He'd seen thick grease applied liberally to metal parts exposed to the weather. Calico Jack kept growling and trying to squirm free.

"Just hold on … we got to get this off. Let me look at that hind end of yours."

He spun the cat around and caught a claw in the hand. A little drop of blood popped out. He ignored it. The raw spot near the cat's hind end was mostly missing fur, but there was a cut that he presumed had come from a fight. The cut was fresh and razor thin like it had been caused by a claw. He took out some ointment from one of the drawers and dabbed it on gently. If it worked on humans, it'd work on cats, he reasoned. Calico Jack hissed at him and tried to leap off the counter.

"Just one more spot."

He swiped the paws and it had been blood on the right leg, but he didn't see any open wounds so he assumed it'd come from the other cat. Once he had him cleaned up, he put the cat down on the floor and observed how he walked. Calico Jack didn't seem any worse for the wear, so he unwrapped another hunk of salmon and set it down on the floor and watched the animal eat.

"We'll both be back to new before you know it," he said.

With that, he found a box of cereal in the cupboard, filled a bowl, dumped on some almond milk and stood there sharing a meal with his buddy.

Feeling parched, he grabbed a bottle of water from the refrigerator and went outside and sat at a table on the deck. He took in a few deep breaths of fresh air and then picked up his cell phone again.

Dr. Rachael Phillip was working at the hospital today. They placed him on hold to track her down. She eventually picked up. She sounded pleasant. He introduced himself.

"I'm familiar with you Deputy. Nurse Blake provided me with a full report. What can I do for you?"

"How is she doing?"

"No change."

"That's unfortunate. I was hoping to speak with her today.

"I'm afraid that won't be possible."

"When might I be able to?"

"That all depends on how she responds to treatment."

"Could you call me if her situation improves?" There was a long silence. "Dr. Phillip? Are you still there?"

"Yes, yes. I'm sorry. I'm in the middle of five things. What was your question again?"

"Would you notify me when she's conscious?"

"I may not allow visitation then…"

"I'll need a statement from her. It shouldn't take long. It's extremely important."

Another silence. "I could have a staff member call. Give me your information."

Following a long, hot shower, a few quick swipes with a razor and change of clothes, he checked in on the cat. The salmon was gone. He checked the windowsill, but Jack was gone. Colefield assumed he was outside. He was surprised when he rounded the corner to find him curled up on the sofa, something that had never occurred before. He figured it was a good omen.

11

Colefield had just returned to the River Patrol to type up his notes on the latest interview and the mysterious character known as the River Rat when he received a text that Jesse was waiting for him at the hospital cafeteria.

The entrance opened into a self-service buffet. Interns and nurses on short breaks darted around gathering sandwiches, fruit, donuts, coffee, whatever they could snatch up, while the rest of the general public wandered about aimlessly killing time. There were large tables of hospital staff. A man sitting alone at another table sort of resembled the picture Colefield had in mind of what the brother looked like. But the man's hair was a different color and much shorter. No one really fit the description. So, he figured he'd grab a cup of coffee, while he waited for the brother to show up. Perhaps he was still upstairs visiting Nicole.

He fell in line behind an attractive woman about his height. She had coal black hair and looked fit. She had on a black knit dress and heels and smelled lavender sweet. She must have sensed that Colefield was staring and turned around.

He immediately noticed her dark eyes. They were the color of coffee liqueur set against high cheek bones and an angular face. Something about her struck him.

"It's like a Black Friday in Starbucks in here, isn't it?" she said, breaking the spell.

"Must be a shift change. What brings you to this lovely place?"

"My sister's upstairs. And you?"

"I'm meeting someone."

"So am I…" She glanced down at the nametag on his tactical vest before facing the front of the line as they approached the cashier. She opened her purse and pulled out a wad of money.

The attendant told her the amount she owed, and she surprised Colefield by saying she wanted to buy the coffee for the deputy standing behind her. Before he could object, the attendant added it to her bill. She paid and moved through to the sitting area.

Colefield followed her. "Thank you. But why did you buy me coffee?"

"You're welcome, deputy," she said, smiling. "Shall we have a seat in the corner?"

"I'm sorry. Do I know you?"

"I'm Jesse Dafoe, Nicole's brother…"

Colefield swallowed hard and looked her over.

"Say that again?"

"I think you heard me correctly the first time."

"You're…" Colefield couldn't finish his sentence.

"Yes. I am. And, I'm sure it was not what you were expecting."

He took it all in. The resemblance was there, stronger than ever and yet he'd missed it completely. Or had he? He certainly hadn't counted on a transvestite or transgender or trans something.

She set her coffee down and put out her hand. "Thank you for getting ahold of me and for what you are doing for my big Sis."

Colefield missed nothing. The way she held her head tilted at her best angle, the guarded look in her eye, the curve of her neck, the rather impressive chest, the large hands and polished nails.

He shook her hand still in shock over the reality that Nicole's brother turned out to be something far different than what he was expecting.

"Does your sister know?"

"Of course. She's been very supportive. I had the surgeries several years ago. Nicole moved to Thailand to be with me. I'll always be grateful that she was there to help me through my transition."

"Surgeries?"

"Snip, snip…"

Colefield needed to change the subject. "Nicole? Have you seen her?"

Jesse's eyes glassed over. "The sun was shining down on her when I entered her room. Look — I am used to hospital rooms and the brutality of her injuries."

Colefield figured Jesse had experienced plenty of traumas just enduring her own surgeries.

Jesse slid her coffee aside and leaned toward Colefield. "I needed to see if she was still in there. We used to play a cat and mouse game as kids. As hard to believe as it is, I was the mouse." Jesse's face twisted into a wry grin. "We developed secret signals to communicate when we were kids. So I whispered something from our games in her ear, she didn't stir or smile but I know she's still in there because she made a purring noise that anyone else would think was a gurgle, but that I recognized as Nicole telling me she was happy as a cat. I think she has a fighting chance."

Colefield rubbed his neck and hoped she was right.

"Does my sex bother you? Be honest."

"You're different than what I was expecting. I'll work on it. Welcome to Portland by the way."

"Thank you." She reached into her purse and pulled out a small black journal like the one Montgomery had found in Nicole's place. The similarity jarred him.

She opened the notebook, thumbed back a few pages, and read over her notes. "In your recorded message, you mentioned there was a witness? Someone who saw the accident?"

"I spoke with the witness. Unfortunately, his story doesn't paint a very clear picture of what happened. He was patrolling the airfield about a quarter of a mile away and so most of what he claims he saw is circumstantial at best. Although, he did provide a nugget of information regarding the possibility of a second vehicle in the vicinity at the time of the accident. He admitted his eye sight isn't what it used to be, but he thinks he saw a second pair of headlights following your sister's car."

"What does that mean? There might be other witnesses?"

"There's something else, too. There may be a third witness — a homeless man. We believe he may live on a boat or possibly be camped out along the river. He may be responsible for saving your sister's life."

Jesse put her notebook down, took a sip of coffee, staring at him, as if she was processing the new information. "The accident happened after dark, right?"

"Around 11:30 p.m."

"Nicole's night vision has never been very good. When she was a girl, she rode her bicycle off an embankment near our house. She broke her leg in three places. She tried crawling but it was too painful for her. So, she saved her strength and lay in the woods over night before authorities could locate her. She's tough as nails. If you notice, she still walks with a slight limp."

Colefield didn't remember a limp. What he did remember were her sexy legs. He picked up his coffee and took a drink. Although he found it a little disturbing to admit, he was drawn to Jesse Dafoe, too.

"You're still in shock, aren't you?" she said.

"Truthfully, kind of. If I hadn't seen the photograph of you as a man ... it wouldn't have been so dramatic."

"That god awful sleazy tennis shot? She still keeps that around?" Jesse fluffed her hair back.

Colefield cleared his throat. "I'm just glad you showed up for your sister. Many times, I've telephoned relatives after an accident and felt their indifference."

"My parents would never show up for me."

"That's more common than you'd believe."

"I'm very curious about this second set of headlights that you mentioned because it doesn't make sense to me. If someone was following behind her, why haven't they come forward? Why didn't they stop and offer help?"

"Could be many reasons. Like if they were drunk and didn't want to get a DUI or they had a warrant out for their arrest … or they caused it."

"So you're saying that maybe this wasn't an accident?"

"Based on the testimony and the data I've been collecting … and mind you, I have no proof yet so don't hold me to this, but I'd bet money that this was no accident."

Jesse reared back and stared at him. "Can your office track down the other car?"

"After we leave here, I'm going to interview a guard at the VA that saw an assault that may be connected to your sister and then take a closer look at her Mercedes to see if there is any evidence to corroborate my theory."

"What you meant to say is — *we* are going to take a closer look at everything? You're stuck with me, deputy. I didn't come all this way for nothing."

"I'll have to check with my Lieutenant first."

Jesse picked up her coffee, took a sip and grimaced. "This stuff is awful."

"Just a notch better than the instant I had this morning. That'd put hair on your chest."

"Well, I certainly won't be drinking any of that."

They looked at each other and laughed as the tension evaporated.

12

The Portland Veteran's Administration Hospital sat on the upper edge of a hillside in Southwest Portland, surrounded by forest. It was a large complex and modern by conventional standards with a winding road leading up to it.

Colefield pulled up to the hospital entrance. "This is where you get out."

Jesse started to object. Colefield held up his hand. "I'm working an angle to your sister's case that involves a different assault in the parking garage here. She was a hospital administrator, named Arlene Hanson. I want you to use your detective skills and see if you can pick up any gossip on her assault. Hang around the bathrooms, lobby, cafeteria — whatever it takes."

"Well I am very good at going undercover. Played a man for years."

"I'll meet you back here when I am done interviewing the guard who witnessed the assault."

Colefield drove his pickup to the guard shack and stopped. He glanced inside, but there didn't appear to be anyone around. He drove into the lot and circled several times until he found an available space on the upper level.

He was impressed how full the lot was. Several seniors with wives or other members of their family at their side, along with some crippled-up men either in wheelchairs or with canes or walkers, sidled toward the hospital entrance. Two young men walking on crutches exited the building passing by signs pointing out where the elevators were located.

Colefield walked through the parking lot noting if there were any security personnel in uniform patrolling the area either on foot on in a vehicle. After a lap around the upper and lower areas and a hike over to the overflow lot, he saw no sign of security, which didn't mean they weren't patrolling. It meant they had limited staff making rounds. He did note security cameras mounted throughout, which might prove invaluable when trying to identify someone assaulted.

When Colefield returned to the guard shack, a heavyset black man was inside cradling a Styrofoam coffee cup. Colefield rapped on the sliding glass window. As the guard spun, Colefield pressed his badge up to the glass. The man frowned, unlatched the window and slid it open.

"Deputy, you damn near gave me a heart attack."

"Sorry. Mind if I ask you a few questions?"

"Just let me take a sip of this brew first. It's always best when it's hot."

Colefield waited. The guard took his time sipping his coffee. When he apparently felt he'd had enough he made eye contact.

"Your name again, deputy?"

"Jason Colefield. Were you here the night the VA Administrator was attacked?"

"I sure was. I found Ms. Hanson."

"Where?"

"In the overflow parking, the one behind you." He opened his guard shack and stepped out. "Back over there," he pointed. "Where that yellow pickup is parked."

"What happened?"

"Her co-workers said she left the office late that night alone. Someone attacked her outside her car. Damn near beat her to death. Whoever did it was one strong SOB. He broke five of her ribs, her arm, her leg, and fractured her skull. Haven't seen that kind of violence in my 30-years."

"Did you get footage of it?"

"Afraid it wasn't much help. Guy wore a hoody. His back was to the cameras. He painted camouflage makeup on his face. The paint had metal flakes mixed in which distorted the video of his features. Bank robbers do that occasionally. That's what the police said. He wasn't some gang banger after a few bucks. This guy knew what he was doing."

"So, it wasn't a robbery?"

"Nope. Her purse was found on the car seat. Apparently, cash and credit cards inside."

"She made it inside her car before he attacked?"

"Didn't get the door locked in time. He smashed her head against the steering wheel, knocked out a few teeth and then dragged her body out of the car and beat the tar out of her."

"Can I see the security tape?"

"I believe the police took the tape with them. You can always ask my boss. He's located on the first floor in room 100."

"Was there any physical evidence left behind?"

"Just hers. Guy wore leather gloves and his arms were covered up. If she did get any scratches in, they weren't deep enough to do us any good. There were no traces of skin under her nails. That's what I was told anyway…"

"Why do you think the attack wasn't mentioned in the newspapers?"

"That was an administrative decision above my pay grade. Somebody felt it was safer for Ms. Hanson if the incident didn't go public. Not until they had more information on the assailant." Just talking about it caused the man's eyes to tear. "He knocked half her teeth out. What kind of animal does that to a sweet young woman? I've been in combat. Served two tours with the 101st Airborne, and I saw some pretty grisly things that I still have nightmares about. But to see a woman like that, covered in blood with her appendages broken like pretzels … and, her face, God all mighty, it was just a rubbery bloody mess when he got through with it."

The guard's hands were trembling and his eyes glassed over. Then he sneezed and swiped at his running nose.

"I hate to be the one to tell you this, but the woman died."

"Oh Lord! That poor, poor, girl."

"Did Ms. Hanson have family?"

"She was a single woman, no children."

"What about a current boyfriend?"

"I didn't know her personally, really. I walked her to her car on a couple of occasions. If I only would have that night. But I had to respond to a car alarm on the second level."

"Was there a break-in?"

"No — the alarm was just going off. Didn't see a soul around."

"Think it was connected? Used as a distraction?"

"Might have been. But we didn't see anything on the tape to corroborate it."

"What do you think the motive for the assault was?"

"Well, funny you'd ask that. Cops did too. Now you would think the attack would have occurred after the Town Hall meeting we had here on Monday night, because we bring on two extra security personnel for those events. We anticipate things might get out of hand. But they didn't that night. That's not to say there weren't some pissed-off folk. These young veterans can get pretty hot-headed. We've had to break up a few brawls in the past, but as I was saying, that night everything went pretty smoothly. No real issues to contend with. Then two nights later, when our guard is down, Ms. Hanson gets attacked, right under our nose. Now you say she's dead."

"Would you mind showing me exactly where it took place?"

"No, course not." The guard led him across the area to the overflow lot on the east side. The yellow pickup that the guard had mentioned was parked across from the spot where the administrator was found.

"It happened right over there where that dark stain is."

The stain was about the size of a kid's blanket. Someone had cleaned up the blood but the floor had not been steam-cleaned and traces were still visible.

Colefield looked for the nearest security camera. The domed-shaped camera lens was mounted at the end of the lot about seven feet up on a concrete wall. It was at a bad angle and would be easy to get around if you were trying.

"Ms. Hanson drove a black Hyundai. I understand they towed it to impound."

"And nothing was stolen? What about a briefcase or files or something she was carrying from work?"

"Nothing was reported missing by the police. Her purse, as I mentioned, was on the passenger seat. Guy didn't even go through it. She had on a nice gold watch and gold earrings. Nothing touched."

"Well, thanks. I appreciate it. I'll go check in with your boss about the tape."

"If you ever catch the bastard, promise me that he'll get what he gave."

13

J esse had been busy. She'd gotten the name of Nicole's boss and her office number. Apparently, Dr. Rosin was willing to do anything she could to assist Nicole's family.

After checking in with security, they rode the elevator to the Psychiatric Ward on the top floor. The locked unit was at the end of the hall. Colefield buzzed the intercom on the wall and waited, looking out the large picture windows at the splendid view of Mt. Hood and Mt. Saint Helens in the distance. They seemed a million light years away.

The intercom squeaked. "Yes, what can I do for you?"

Colefield pressed his credentials up to the glass. "We'd like to speak with Dr. Nicole Dafoe's supervisor."

"That will be Dr. Rosin. Is she expecting you?"

"Yes," replied Jesse.

"It's been a busy day for her. One moment, please."

After a few minutes, the door buzzed open. A mechanical voice announced: "Please follow the yellow line to the nursing station."

Colefield pushed the heavy door back breathing in a harsh antiseptic odor. He suppressed a cough as the metal door locked behind them. The painted yellow line on the corridor floor reminded him of the Multnomah County Jail. There were rooms, both on the right and left. He spotted a teenager crouched in the corner by a drinking fountain clutching an IPod and mumbling gibberish to herself. She had purple hair and wore a hospital gown with pink socks poking out from beneath. Every so often, she would scratch at her wrist wrapped in fresh bandages. Another patient walked by in a faded hospital robe opened in back — a tall male, thin, pale skinned and probably twentyish. His hairless white buttocks hung out for the world to see. He seemed to be in a drug induced fog. He paced back and forth, repeatedly running a limp hand through his unkempt hair. A nurse walked out of one of the rooms and went over to him. She retied the string that held his robe closed in back and then led him to the drinking fountain and handed him some pills and a paper cup. She watched over him while he took his medication.

The nursing station was in the center of the ward. Like a guard tower, the area was circular with glass windows on all sides. The desk had a view of each room. Colefield figured maybe twenty beds total. Some of them had their doors open and he heard TV's blaring. He heard a scream coming from a room down on the end where two male nurses calmly entered and closed the door. In another room, he saw an Asian man sitting up in bed, glued to a blacked-out television screen, laughing uncontrollably.

Together they walked up to the nursing station. Colefield put his mouth near an amplified speaker box. The attendant behind the counter was scribbling some notes in a file. "I'll be right with you," she said before either of them had time to speak.

There were cameras everywhere and a large monitor with live feed. Colefield hadn't noticed it at first but Jesse pointed out that someone had left a trail of urine in the hallway. Within moments, a janitor appeared. Using a key card to open the locked doors, he wheeled his mop bucket into the area and began to clean up the mess.

"Yes, how may we be of help?"

"You were going to provide us directions to Dr. Rosin's office?" Jesse spoke up.

"She has someone with her. It'll just be a moment."

Colefield stared down at the women's hands. She was a nail bitter. "How many patients do you have here on a regular basis?"

"The unit can accommodate twenty-four. We're at capacity and short staffed this week. It's a little chaotic now."

The receptionist's telephone rang. She picked it up, spoke to someone briefly, and hung up.

"She'll see you now. Down the hall, last office on your left. If the door is shut, just knock and announce yourself."

As they stepped up to the closed door and got ready to knock, it flung open. An angry man stormed out. He was built, in his mid-twenties, short dark hair, square jaw, and broad shoulders. He had on a tight-fitting T-shirt that showed off his muscles.

He looked right through them as he strode down the hall. Colefield recognized the guy from somewhere but couldn't place him. He wore a collegiate ring. Maybe he played football somewhere. He watched him make for the exit.

"Should we give her a minute to get her shit together?" Jesse suggested.

"I expect they're used to this 'shit' as you call it, happening all the time." Colefield paused, recalling one of his own particularly violent outbursts during a counseling session. "A couple of years ago, that could have been me." Coalfield knocked on the door before Jesse had time to respond.

Dr. Rosin glanced up from the stack of files. "Sorry about my last visitor. He left rather angry."

"Yes, he looked upset," Jesse said.

"His brother is a patient of ours. He's just concerned about his welfare. Take a seat. I'll be right with you."

After a few moments, she put her pen down, blew her nose, and looked up. "Now, you're here to discuss Dr. Dafoe, is that correct?"

"Yes."

"I'm so sorry to hear about her accident. She's an excellent employee. She has been with us for a little over two months. She was hired as a temporary contractor to fill the gap in our little budget fiasco and to help ease our overcrowding issues. Is she going to be all right?"

"The last I heard, she's still in a coma," Jesse said.

"What happened exactly?"

Colefield cleared his throat. "Our office is still looking into it."

"Well, how can I help you?"

"What exactly does Dr. Dafoe do here?" he asked.

"She is a psychiatrist who counsels PTSD patients with lingering mental health issues. She has full prescriptive privileges as well as the ability to assign additional treatment options if she deems it necessary. Her job is to get the returning veterans assimilated into civilian life as quickly as possible."

"Have there been any problems recently?"

"These are young vets that pass through here. Chaos and outbursts occur occasionally but nothing recently requiring security to intervene."

"I'm Dr. Dafoe's sister, Jesse." She extended her hand. "What I just saw would seem to warrant intervention."

"With her accident happening so soon after the assault of one of our administrators, we've discussed the impact it might be having on patients and co-workers." She paused. "Do you think the administrator's death and Dr. Dafoe's accident are related?"

"Possibly," Colefield said. "And we think there may be more. That is why access to her caseload files would be helpful."

"I think you know the answer to that as well as I do. The one thing the DOD does do well is respect the confidentiality of our veterans."

"Even if it puts everyone associated with them in danger?" Jesse asked.

Colefield cut in. "You know anyone who would have wanted to kill these two women?"

Rosin sighed. "People who come in here need some serious care. We have a staff of eight — sorry — now six — to handle this workload. You saw our waiting room. We see two hundred patients a day." Rosin took a deep breath. "It's killing us."

Rosin opened the lid of her laptop and began typing. "You know these soldiers, her patients, many are homeless. A few are on disability but barely scraping by. They have lost ties to the community and their families. Their military records are the most complete picture we have of them."

Rosin turned the laptop around. "Here is the list of Dr. Dafoe's' recent schedule."

Jesse leaned in. "She was busy. There are only initials in the time slots? And what do those red dots by some of the names mean?"

"Red means dangerous."

Jesse stared at the screen. "How dangerous?"

"Someone that is calculating, fearless and remorseless. A sociopath…"

"Half the names have red dots."

Looking worried, Jesse glanced over at Colefield.

"Don't read too much into this. Each clinician has their own interpretations."

"You think it's a veteran?" Colefield asked.

Dr. Rosin hesitated. "The swiftness and precision with which Ms. Hanson was beaten all seems directed at sending a clear and serious message. This person could have just killed her but they chose to make her endure tremendous suffering. It could be a random attack, but as I understand, robbery wasn't the motive. Either the person was deeply disturbed with an encounter they had with the administrator or has an overall grudge against the VA. And I would be surprised if the police catch him any time soon."

"Why?" Jesse asked.

"My doctorate is in Psychology. My internship was at Sing Sing. I got an opportunity to learn from some of the best." She focused her eyes on Jesse. "In the case of our attacker, he left behind no physical evidence. I also believe he is so skilled at controlling his rage that it fuels him, gives him special powers if you will. But the trigger mechanism that keeps it from going off loses its resilience. Triggers can be anything from a smell, like cordite, or even a pattern of speech which triggers a painful past event. One of the prisoners I interviewed lost control when he observed a grown man stroke a child's hand."

Colefield interrupted. "About Dr. Dafoe, it may be nothing or it could be something unrelated to her work, but the night of her accident, she asked if I did bodyguard work for hire. At first, I didn't make much of it. We'd just met, and she didn't go into detail. Did she mention if she was feeling threatened by one of her patients?"

"There was a recent phone message from her. She needed to discuss something but didn't provide details. I'm ashamed to say, I never got back to her."

"Can you help me requisition her patient files?" Colefield asked.

"Follow me and I'll put in a request. Just don't expect anything to come of it." As Rosin stood and led Colefield to the door, she turned to Jesse. "I trust you can occupy yourself for a few moments while we're gone."

Before the door clicked shut, Jesse was already moving toward Dr. Rosin's computer. She flopped down in front of the keyboard but before she could search the patient database, the screen went black. The only way to reopen it was with a password. Jesse began to search her office.

After Colefield and the doctor returned, Jesse's demeanor had changed. They thanked Rosin and left. Out in the hallway, she uttered: "I didn't know sis was dealing with these types of mental patients — all capable killers. I'm sure she is still in danger. Please take me back to the hospital."

"Were you able to get into Rosin's computer?"

"No."

"What about a printout or photograph of her schedule?"

"It was just initials and those horrible dots…" Jesse let out a heavy sigh. "Jason, I'm sorry. I'm so rattled by all this. I'll go back and ask for it."

Jesse turned back toward the door. Colefield put his hand on her shoulder. "She gave us our chance. It's protected information. She took a risk. Don't worry about it. We'll find something."

Colefield last saw Jesse parked in a chair outside her sister's hospital room, a look of determination on her face and a concealed .38 strapped to her ankle.

"I'll Uber over to my hotel and check myself in later," she said.

"Anything I can do for you in the meantime?"

"We know somebody tried to kill her. Now, I'd like you to find the homeless man who saved her."

14

It was late with fine midnight dew glistening on the tall grass as Colefield stopped to catch his breath along the fence. His shift was over but his work wasn't. If the guy was hunting tonight, he figured it would be about the right time to spot him.

Before he left the office, he'd checked in with Jesse. She'd left the hospital depressed. Nicole was still showing little progress. After Ubering to her hotel, she'd broken into a bottle of scotch and was having a stiff drink. Colefield said he'd see her in the morning and signed off letting her know he was going to hang around the airport for a while before calling it a night.

"Be careful, Jason," she said.

He felt tired, hungry, weary from the long hours and lack of sleep.

With night-vision binoculars slung around his neck and the comfort of his Glock strapped to his hip he stopped for a moment, stared toward the empty field and the deserted runway in the distance. Something rustled in the grass up ahead. It startled him. He reached for his weapon and then stopped when a beady-eyed possum poked his grizzled white-face out of the brush. Snarling a jagged fang, it waddled off toward a ditch ahead, dragging its hairless tail over the ground. The animal had taken him by surprise. His chest was beating a click faster. He took a few deep breaths and exhaled slowly, taking in the dark surroundings.

Using binoculars, he scanned beyond the fence and along the vast area near the runways. There was a utility road that ran along Port Property, which is where the guards patrolled. He didn't see any headlights in either direction, just the red, blue, and yellow glow of runway lights.

He settled in and waited.

Time grinded by. A breeze kicking up off the river blew in a murky, earthy scent, tinged with dead fish heads.

He had trouble focusing. One of the binocular lenses fogged. He wiped it off with his sleeve and then took another scan of the area.

Still nothing…

His cell phone chimed. He snatched it from his pocket. A text came in from Bart. The blue screen was like a beacon in the dark. Chances were he'd just blown his cover.

Bart forgot to tell him earlier that someone named Captain Montgomery had called about cracking the code. That was the extent of the message.

Colefield felt a pang of excitement, silenced his cell, and shoved it back into his pocket. Faint hope lived — maybe even a second chance of finding something, which was more than he had a moment earlier…

He reached for the binoculars when he heard what sounded like a twig snapping behind him. His flashlight was on the ground beside him. He stuck out a hand when he heard a deep male voice behind him.

"Just leave it there. And don't turn around." The voice resonated power and authority.

"I'm a deputy," Colefield said.

"I know who you are. Keep your hand away from your holster and relax. I'm not here to harm you."

"Who are you?"

"I've learned quite a lot about you in the last few days."

"I wish I could say the same about you. I presume you are who they call 'River Rat'."

"How is the woman?"

"Alive. Why do you care?"

The man hesitated. "I did what I was trained to do."

"Did you? Why not come forward and tell us your side of the story. She has a sister who would like some answers."

"I'm not much of a talker."

"You're a material witness. You're smart enough to know I have a legal right to interview you in a proper setting."

"I'm not stepping foot inside your office."

"Well, this is as good a place as any…"

Colefield spun around to look at the man. The moment he did, the man flashed a powerful laser light into his eyes that temporarily left him sightless. Only a blurred silhouette burned into his memory of a medium-built man wearing worn BDU's packing a sniper rife slung over his shoulder. Camo makeup smeared the features of his face.

"You don't listen well," he said.

"I'm a slow learner…"

"And a smartass. You'll walk away from here unharmed and with some valuable information if you keep your head."

"You've got my attention. But shine that light in my face one more time and we'll see who walks away unharmed."

"OK — tough guy. You need to be looking for a brown Hummer. Newer model. I caught a glimpse of the driver but I can't place him. He's got one of those faces that you recognize immediately but can't recall from where. Give me a few days and maybe I'll be able to come up with a name. For now, I suggest you look for the vehicle."

"You get a plate number?"

"Nope."

"You're sure it was a Hummer and not a Humvee?"

"Could have been either. I was more focused on the woman in the river."

"You come to my office, I could call in a sketch artist, might help us."

"You heard me before…"

"Yeah, right. A woman's lying in a hospital bed and you've got lofty principles. What else are you willing to tell me about that night?"

"Just look for the vehicle…"

"What's your name?"

Colefield's vision started to return. He wanted a clear look at this guy but he couldn't risk a second blast to his eyes. Whatever laser the guy had was powerful enough to do permanent damage.

After an awkward silence, Colefield said: "Fine … then how can I reach you if I find out something?"

Only more silence…

Colefield weighed his options and listened for breathing or anything that would tell him the man was still standing behind him. After another long pause, he swallowed hard and turned around.

River Rat had vanished.

15

The following morning, July 2nd, Colefield finally rousted Montgomery. After his encounter with the River Rat, he had pounded on Montgomery's door several times but either rum or fatigue had gotten the best of the old pirate. Colefield could hear him snoring through an open second-floor window. He called out his name but got no reply. So, he let him sleep it off.

Now he was back at the door and had only knocked once when Montgomery's frizzly face peered around the north corner of the houseboat. His eyes had a devilish glow about them as he re-tied his tattered bathrobe. His landlord had apparently been tinkling into the river again while observing a neighbor. He waved Colefield over. Colefield joined him and saw the silhouette of a naked woman through a bathroom window.

"A new morning pastime?" Colefield turned away.

"If only I had known, old boy, I wouldn't have spent all these years perusing porno magazines on the john when I could have been watching her."

"You mean, stalking her."

Montgomery snorted at the remark and went back inside.

Colefield followed him toward his kitchen table where he spent most of his days scribbling notes, collecting anything related to weaponry and plotting his next caper.

"Have a seat," he said. "I'm going upstairs to put on something more respectable."

"I heard you cracked the code."

"All in due time, old boy…"

"You have any coffee made?"

"There's a jar of instant on the counter. You know where the cups are."

And with that, Montgomery inched his way up the rickety circular staircase to the level above. Colefield could hear him banging around in drawers while he moved to the kitchen and searched the cupboards for a clean coffee cup. Montgomery had a special faucet for hot water by the sink, hooked up to its own small heater where boiling water was instantly dispensed. Colefield shoveled in two heaping teaspoons of the coffee crystals and held it under the tap. The aroma hit him at the same moment as the smell of a stinking garbage sack on the floor behind him.

Colefield stepped back and took a sip of the bitter coffee. He set the cup down, picked up the garbage and shoved it inside a new trash bag he pulled from the cupboard. Afterwards he rearranged a few stacks of yellow tablets off one of the chairs and shuffled a pile of gun magazines, clearing a spot at the table.

He saw the black journal lying across the table on a stack of papers with sticky notes stuck between the pages. A yellow pad with all sorts of scribbling lay beside it, diagrams mostly with letters and sets of strange symbols and little dots.

He went to reach for the tablet when a cane thudded the wood floor above him. "Put that down!" Montgomery's voice barked. "No peaky-pooh!"

"I see you got your security cameras working again…"

"Can't be too careful. Never know what kind of riffraff might wander in."

Montgomery hobbled downstairs in baggy blue jeans and a faded NRA T-shirt. He approached the table, extended his stiff leg, dropped down into his favorite chair and let out a groan. He put on a pair of smudged reading glasses.

"Your sexy Ms. Dafoe is quite an encrypter," he said in a raspy voice. "Not only were her notes in shorthand, but she utilized a secondary cipher for the juicy parts."

Colefield begrudgingly admired Montgomery's abilities. "Go ahead."

"First some bad news ... this notebook of hers was recent. Just the last three weeks. She may have others."

"I'll take what I can get."

Montgomery paused and gathered his thoughts. "There are two tried and true methods to creating a secret language. I suppose you may have learned that in the Navy. But let me explain it again ... in case you have forgotten."

Colefield stared at Montgomery's notes.

"Two methods, old boy, two methods. We're talking codes and ciphers. The difference is not worth diddling over. For our purpose, codes are words substituted for other words and ciphers are letters substituted for other letters. One of the least known and probably the most effective in history was used in WWII. It was a secret dictionary of Navajo code words and numerous words for military terms. The Army recruited 29 Navajos back in '42 for a secret project. They were tasked with creating this dictionary and all military code words to be used on the battlefield. Then the poor bastards had to commit it all to memory before being assigned to a Marine unit serving in the Pacific. They were called the Navajo Code Talkers. They could decipher messages in the heat of battle in about 20 seconds. Before that it took 30 minutes to decode messages with a machine. In all about 500 were recruited for this duty. Without them, the marines would never have taken Iwo Jima. The Japanese were blindsided by their talents. And the code was never broken."

"Did you decipher her code?"

"Our neighbor didn't use the Navajo language. She wasn't that sophisticated. No, Ms. Dafoe used a diagrammatic cipher, used by many children. It utilizes a tic-tac-toe chart and two

X's. It took me a little over two hours to figure it out but I'm not the man I used to be. Nonetheless, you can't fool an old Marine with cryptography training."

Montgomery picked up his yellow tablet, thumbed through a number of pages, tore them off and handed them across the table. "Here's the conversion. As I said, the ciphering of the names was more difficult because she only used initials."

"So, we don't have names?"

"Not in the Biblical sense."

Colefield remained positive. The first two pages looked like nothing but medical gibberish. He was about to say something when he turned to the third page and got the meat of it. He read through a total of twelve pages and then set the stack down and began to formulate a picture in his mind.

"Can I trust you to return the journal on your own?" Colefield stood up. "I'm going to hang on to your cryptography notes."

"Be my guest. I was simply trying to be of service."

"You're certain you can't put together names for me?"

"Unless I missed something. She seemed content to use initials. Conceivably, she could be using the letter of the first and last name. JR, for instance, could stand for John Rice. Or, she could use the first initial of the first name and the last initial of the last name. In that case, JR could stand for John Winger. There are innumerable combinations. I will keep at it. At least you have three psychological profiles. Now it's up to you."

"Have you ever known someone to use a combination of shorthand and cryptography?"

"No. But she was entering the Lion's Den with these Vets. Their confessions could be damning if someone got ahold of it. I'm sure she did her best to protect their confidentiality."

"Mind if I sit here a minute and reread?"

Tracking down the bastard who tried to kill Nicole, as Montgomery had said, wouldn't be easy. Colefield studied Montgomery's notes. Her deciphered shorthand pinpointed mental cases that left her worried for her safety. Down to the last bit of information, she only used initials for identification. And who knew if these initials meant anything or were just another code.

The JR notes seemed the most thorough. Montgomery had used it as his reference, which probably meant that he felt some connection. Another two which also drew plenty of attention were BN and ZE.

From the beginning, Nicole had tried various clinical methodologies with JR but nothing seemed to be working. As a last attempt at a breakthrough, she invited his younger brother into therapy. He hadn't been a Vet. He had attended college on a football scholarship and seemed like a good role model. At this stage, she was running out of ideas.

The plan had failed almost from the beginning. On the surface, JR had served a total of eight years in the military and was awarded a number of medals. The younger brother had been a star player in college. Both had succeeded in dangerous jobs. JR was a bomb disposal technician for the Air Force while his younger brother had been a linebacker and had avoided injury. The two saw each other occasionally during this time. JR had seen combat and had admitted to having bouts of depression and anger but that was not uncommon given what he'd been through. His younger brother admitted to having his own issues with anger, especially after not making the draft picks.

Wherever a note was entered she referred to the younger brother as YB. Their lives took drastic changes after JR's military career ended and his brother's college days were done. JR's PTSD took over and he had trouble acclimating in society and had become homeless. After college YB went on to start up his own company, something to do with demolition work, and on the surface, gave the appearance that he was content, adjusted, and had finally accepted not making the NFL draft pick.

But that was not the whole story. Nicole's notes indicated she had learned something troubling about YB's past.

Something was scratching at the back of Colefield's mind…

The other two initials BN and ZE were as different as day and night. BN had been an Army Infantryman. On his first assignment to Iraq the Humvee he was riding in hit an IED and was blown off the road. All four soldiers inside the vehicle had been severely wounded. It was early in the days of the war. Some of the Humvee's armor plating was substandard then. Three of the four soldiers in the vehicle were unable to escape. BN had some shrapnel wounds on his face and chest but compared to the other men, he was in the best shape. He crawled out under gunfire and made it to cover. But before he could help his fellow soldiers, a well-placed bullet struck the fuel tank and the Humvee caught fire. The three soldiers trapped inside died. BN had severe PTSD and guilt over seeing his friends burned alive in front of him. Since returning to the States, he'd had several run-ins with the police for assault.

The person with the ZE initials was a female medic formerly assigned to the 142nd Medical Squadron. She was an Air National Guard Member on her second tour in Afghanistan. Twenty-three-years-old and engaged to be married upon her return to the states. The helicopter she was flying in evacuating wounded soldiers came under gunfire and had to set down in hostile territory. Some of the passengers aboard were injured during the abrupt landing. ZE, herself banged up and shaken, kept her head in the game and managed to fight off dissidents for a while. Several shot their way in, dragged her bullet riddled body from the chopper and raped her repeatedly, leaving her for dead.

Having given up all hope of survivors, a team of USAF Combat Controllers swept in and with the help of Apache gunfire decimated the attackers. ZE struggled with uncontrollable panic attacks, a heightened fear of enclosed spaces, and physical and emotional scars. Antipsychotic drugs kept her so numb that she was unable to connect with family or friends. Her fiancée couldn't take her unending bouts of depression and anger and walked away from the relationship. Going against her doctor's recommendation she quit taking her antidepressants. Two days later she was arrested for civil disobedience at a peace rally. At her last visit with Dr. Dafoe she admitted to having an alcohol problem and felt she needed to be admitted into rehab.

That all three of these individuals were potentially very dangerous was clear. However, there was no definitive connection to Ms. Dafoe's accident. To get a judge to go along with a request for a complete client list of all her patients, he'd need a hell of a lot more proof. He could imagine the Judge saying: "The streets are filled with dangerous people. This isn't enough. Bring me something…"

These appeared to be her final journal entries. She may have had other notebooks stashed in her office. He would need a subpoena to find them.

As Colefield walked up the marina ramp to the parking lot, his mind was overloaded with fresh data and swirling with images of flaming Humvees and crashing helicopters. He tried to suppress the imagery long enough to get a clear thought. He had completely forgotten to tell Montgomery about the River Rat; he would have found it amusing. He thought about going back but decided against it.

That's when he felt he was being watched…

He set the garbage sack down and glanced around. The dock was quiet normally. And the residents rarely took their boats out of their slips until the weekend. There were no water craft on the river. So why did he feel the goose bumps up his neck? That eerie sense someone with intent of doing harm was lurking.

He took another look to be certain. Everything was quiet, even the blackbirds in the trees had stopped chirping.

It had been the silencing of the birds that alerted him that something was amiss.

Internalizing too much of Dr. Dafoe's journal, had probably been the cause of his paranoia. Her words gave fear a strong hold. He brushed it off and continued up the ramp. Then a weird sensation followed — a lyric, really — an old David Bowie song. The message lodged in his head how they sometimes do and wouldn't go away.

It went something like this: "Paranoia will destroy ya … paranoia will destroy ya …"

Across town, his unease finally subsided. Before then he kept telling himself that the paranoia had been triggered by Dr. Dafoe's short yet descriptive entries that he'd re-read again in his truck, before leaving the marina parking lot. The doctor had felt the same acute sense of being followed as he just had. It probably stemmed from her confession in her journal that she had been treading a very thin line in treatment. Her notes had indicated she believed she was being stalked but couldn't prove it. She knew her patients were capable of violent outbursts but she hadn't sought counsel. After JR confided that he had been on a special bomb squad, had killed innocent Afghanis with some of his devices, had lost two things in his life that he couldn't get over — his own fiancé when she was disarming an IED that exploded in front of him. Then, two weeks later, his beloved bomb dog, *their* beloved bomb dog, Lucy. Intel indicated the building may have been booby-trapped by terrorists. That's why his CO had sent in Lucy first. Everyone waited. And then waited some more. Lucy never came out. She had been his only anchor left after losing his fiancé. Despite being ordered to evacuate the area immediately, he refused. His fellow soldiers had to drag him away when he disobeyed orders and attempted to enter the building to look for his beloved German shepherd. "It would have been a suicide mission," his CO later wrote in his file, back at base headquarters. It was the final event that had sent the soldier over the edge.

The CO had put the letter into the man's official file, indicating he was unfit for further duty. Because there was such a shortage of qualified bomb squad experts overseas, the letter had not been given proper attention. A month later, the same CO was out on maneuvers with his team and had a mishap. He'd stepped on an IED after being told the area was clear. It was suspected and yet never proven that one of the members of his unit was responsible.

It was all there in her ciphered notes — this dark and tortured individual named JR who spiraled down into hell. His implication in the CO's death was clear as was his lack of remorse. Dr. Dafoe had tried to get him to take an anti-psychotic drug but he refused. His condition had worsened. Every sight and sound had become amplified. The former soldier couldn't face reality, not after all the death and destruction, some of which he'd caused. Returning after spending endless weeks isolated out in the wild, he had developed such an acute sense of hearing that even the slightest movement could send him spinning out of control. He was unable to sort through the onslaught of urban sounds, the barrage of noise that struck him from every direction. It was only alone in nature where he found some peace. It reminded him of a happier time with his fiancé, with their dog Lucy, and when he felt his life had meaning.

The other entries in her journal pointed out how BN and ZE were loose cannons, dangerous, unpredictable and suicidal because they felt they had nothing left to live for. Nicole had begun to fear for her safety. That had been her final journal entry.

He texted Jesse that he was running late but headed her way.

Within ten minutes, he rumbled up to the front entrance of the hotel and found a parking spot. He turned off the engine, but left the radio on. A bluesy tune by The Norman Sylvester Band was playing. He listened to the gutsy lyrics and made a note to catch the Boogie Cat the next time he played at Clyde's.

After five minutes, he texted Jesse again and was about to get out of the truck to go see what was keeping her when he caught sight of her out of the corner of his eye, darting across the street, juggling a holder with cups of coffee in one hand and a small brown paper bag in the other. He leaned over and popped the passenger door open.

Jesse jumped inside, handing off the coffee. "Timing is everything!" she said cheerfully. "I figured you for a guy who likes it straight but I've got some cream and sugar in my pocket if you need it. And I didn't know what flavor of bagel you liked so I had to improvise. You have a choice between onion or cinnamon raisin."

"Onion, thanks. Have you checked on Nicole?"

Jesse nodded. "No change yet, but she is still on a truck load of pain killers. They're still pumping fluids in her but they are hopeful she may regain consciousness."

"Just because she is conscious doesn't mean she will be able to help."

"What do you mean?"

"Memory is a strange thing. It might come back in bits and pieces, or all at once."

"Or not at all..." Jesse's mood flatlined.

They sat in the cab of the truck and ate breakfast. Neither of them spoke much. They seemed content to just sip steaming coffee and chew down on the doughy bagels.

Colefield's cell rang.

"Harvey! What's up?"

"What are you doing right now?" His voice sounded troubled.

"Sitting in front of the Mark Spenser Hotel eating a bagel with Jesse."

"I had to settle for a piece of whole grain toast and a poached egg. Wife's got me on some new diet to lower my blood pressure. The thought of it sends my BP soaring through the roof."

"Something else you wanted to share?"

"Who's Jesse?"

"The sister of Dr. Dafoe — I told you about her."

"Don't get pissy … get over to the Portland VA as soon as possible."

"I was heading to work with Jesse."

"I think you're going to want to see this. We found a body — one of your good doctor's patients. You may want to leave the 'he/she' in the truck."

Colefield ignored the remark. "Where's the body?"

"Near the parking structure. Take the main road to the VA. You'll see us. Looks like a circus around here."

"Ten minutes."

The cell went dead. Colefield laid it down on the seat between them. "Change of plans," he said to Jesse. "It may be connected to Nicole."

*   *   *

When the old pickup was about to reach the entrance to the VA Hospital, Detective Feinstein stepped out of the wooded area and flagged Colefield over to the shoulder. Ahead were several patrol cars blocking one lane of Terwilliger Drive and the VA's own security team blocking the entrance to the hospital. A KGW news van was parked along the shoulder. A cameraman and reporter were set up along the hillside just beyond the guards taking footage of the crime scene area.

Colefield rolled down his window. Detective Feinstein walked over. "You made good time," Harvey said.

"V-8 still has a little juice left in her. Jesse, meet Detective Harvey Feinstein."

Jesse faked a smile. "Hello Detective."

"Hello, Jesse. It's a little messy over there. You should probably stay here."

"Don't let my looks deceive you. I was once a Chief Warrant Officer aboard the USS Typhoon. An RPG splattered seven of my fellow sailor's body parts across the ship's deck. I was charged with collecting what was left of them."

Feinstein raised his brow then turned to Colefield. "You should probably move your truck to the other side of the road. Jesse, you keep an eye on the reporters and make sure they stay out of our way."

After Colefield parked, he walked up the hill to rejoin Feinstein.

"A jogger found her about seven this morning. Medical examiner determined the time of death last night, eleven pm at the latest. A body lying in the woods overnight ... well, you'll see what I mean. We suspect some raccoons or rodents picked her apart. She's missing a portion of her face. C'mon, follow me ... and watch your step."

They crossed a small ditch and then began to climb a bank of man-made steps leading up to a remote section of the hospital. Higher up on the hillside, the blue concrete parking structure and VA buildings could be seen.

The pair trudged through over-hanging limbs and fallen branches and came to a small clearing. The victim was lying on her back in the dirt. She looked to be in her mid-twenties, wearing jeans, an Oregon Ducks T-shirt, and hiking boots. The left side of her shirt was torn revealing severe bruising on the neck and shoulders.

For a brief second, Colefield had an image of Jill lying there. She was about the same size as the victim and even the hair was the same color and cut. She was always out jogging late at night after closing the bar, which left him feeling uncomfortable knowing what he did about all the whackos out there.

Blood was everywhere, like Harvey had said. And the wildlife had chewed at parts of her flesh. They had started with the lips and eyes probably because of the moisture and then moved on to the arms. Her neck had deep gouges of missing flesh. One of her upper front teeth had broken off, piercing the lip. Her right eye socket had been crushed. Literally, someone had beaten her to death. The splattering pattern on the ground and on the branches suggested her attacker may have used a heavy object to beat her, or a pair of strong fists.

Colefield walked past the body, careful not to disturb any evidence while he took a closer look.

Feinstein stood beside him. "A mess, ain't she? We've talked with security. They don't have cameras in this area. She did have identification on her. She's a veteran. We think she was on her way to the hospital last night to have a regular group counseling session with Nicole and two other vets. Per Dr. Rosin, none of the members in her group were notified that their usual therapy meeting was canceled. Her group usually meets weekly from 7 to 9 pm in a private room on the sixth floor. Dr. Rosin was kind enough to provide us with everyone's information since this victim's death could be connected. We tracked a James Riker through his brother. He's at a cabin on the Sandy River. The younger brother, Christian, told us he usually drives him to his appointments, hangs around until he's finished and drives him home. They live together. We searched DMV and the older brother hasn't had a vehicle registered in his name since his discharge from service. Christian indicated he did a couple tours in Afghanistan. And is pretty messed up…"

"Is his license current?"

"Let me finish. The guy was officially removed from the program last week. Rosin said she didn't know that he'd had maxed out his allotted benefits. Veterans in counseling are allowed only so many visits with a therapist. Once they reach their limit, it's over. They must request a formal hearing to petition a benefit increase, or get someone with authority to put in a request. The formal process can take months to clear administration. The therapist can make a request on their behalf, so can the boss. In this case, the guy lost on both accounts. Rosin said Christian came into her office several days back and threw a fit. We've flagged him and the brother as persons of interest. This murder and the killing of the VA administrator both show signs of extreme violence."

Colefield looked down the hillside at Jesse. "I may have bumped into this Christian coming out of Rosin's office. Jesse was with me."

"There's something else. The other member of the group, a 27-year-old white single male, has been living in a fleabag hotel downtown. We sent a patrolman to his last known address. He's vacated his room. The manager said he just disappeared. Since leaving the military he's been in and out of jail on drug and assault charges and in and out of shelters. To his credit, the guy did show up at the normal time and was sent home. We just don't know now where 'home' is. Or, if we can tie him to this mess."

"Would his initials be BN?"

"Today might be a good day for you to buy a lottery ticket. Yes, his name is Bob Nelson."

"And the other guy? Is he an 8-year veteran?" Colefield was feeling gratitude toward Montgomery and a little smug. "Served several tours in Afghanistan with an Army Civil Engineering unit? Worked bomb squad? Discharged a little over a year ago? Initials JR? That sound, about right?"

"That could be James Riker — brother of Christian Riker, who I just told you about."

"Are the victim's initials ZE? A former flight medic, served with the 142nd Air National Guard? Was awarded a Silver Star?"

Feinstein stepped back from the body into a clearing and stared at him. "Name's Zoey Elliot, 25, single white female. One theory is that Ms. Elliot was taking a familiar shortcut through the woods." He pointed toward the route that continued up the wooded area and connected to a road leading to the hospital's entrance. "It was a nice evening. Maybe she was running a late for her meeting and wanted to slice off ten minutes or so. Or maybe she's just the type of girl who liked to take risks."

"Or, maybe she likes nature," Jesse's appearance nearby startled the men. "Or needed some more time to get her head together." Jesse picked a ladybug from her hair. "What? Didn't a reporter head this direction?"

"Stay where you are, Jesse," Feinstein said.

Colefield faced Feinstein. "You have an address for her?"

"We do."

"What about a vehicle?"

"She has one registered to her. A 1990 Jeep Wrangler."

"And we're sure she didn't drive last night?"

"I had security sweep the lot. Her car is not here. I believe she took the bus. The Tri Met stop is just down the hill."

"Still, why not take the bus all the way to the main entrance?" Colefield asked. "Why get off and walk?"

"She wasn't afraid," Jesse said. "After what she went through, who would be? She probably took this path every time she came to the VA."

"Point taken," Colefield said. "So, I'm going with the theory that she ran into her killer here, who just happened to be waiting for her. Either that or someone got off the bus with her and waited until they were out of sight to assault her."

Feinstein pulled out his cell phone and placed a call to Tri Met telling Colefield he'd see if he could track down the driver who worked the Terwilliger route.

Jesse paced back and forth while the others worked. After a moment, she stopped and pointed to something lying off the beaten track near her feet in the thick brush. Something the cops had overlooked. "What's that?"

Colefield saw the shiny reflection. He walked over to take a closer look. Underneath some brush the necks of several pint-sized Vodka bottles glittered in the sunlight. They had been stashed over the course of weeks or months, he figured. Two looked fresh, like they'd been dumped there recently. Both had new labels. They hadn't been exposed to the elements long.

Feinstein called over one of the lab techs to collect the bottles.

"Let me add a few thoughts," Colefield said. "Let's say, the victim just used this place to unwind before group. Maybe alone. Maybe not. Maybe she imbibed after group. Hell, you could hardly blame her, given what she'd gone through."

"And someone knew about this little rendezvous area?" Feinstein asked. "And it wasn't random?"

"That's right."

"I tend to agree."

"You think one of the group members did this?" Jesse asked.

"It's a good place to start."

"So, let's say my theory holds water. If Ms. Elliot did make a habit of showing up with booze on her breath it might not win over the heart of the good doctor. My bet is she came here afterwards. Keep her secret hidden from the others. Or, maybe someone from group joined her. That's not a big stretch…"

"You're not much of a vodka drinker, are you?" Jesse said. "Vodka has little odor. With a few breath mints or chewing gum, presto, the scent is gone! Not even my sister, as clever as she is, could pick up the scent. So maybe Detective Feinstein is correct. Maybe she came here first."

"Either way, we agree on this point. She's used this route before." Feinstein nodded. "Then what's the motive for beating her to death? That's the question. This doesn't appear to be a random killing. If one of her fellow soldiers killed her, then perhaps Nicole was onto the suspect. That might have been why she wanted a bodyguard."

Colefield looked over at Jesse as the technician carried the empty Vodka bottles away in a tagged bag.

Feinstein's stomach let out a growl. "This diet is hell."

Colefield said, "Let's say, for amusement purposes, she gets a little rummy one night after her meeting. She starts making out with someone from the group. Maybe she's interested in both guys? They start meeting here after group. Drink a little, mess around a little. The killer starts to feel something again. Then she ends it. And he decides to beat her to death because it's just one more disappointment in life."

"Ms. Elliot doesn't sound like the type. If I may," Jesse interrupted, "making out with a guy might be the furthest thing from her mind."

"Okay, then what about rape?" Colefield said.

Feinstein shook his head. "No, her jeans aren't all muddy or ripped open. Her shirt is still on, not pulled back over her head to secure her arms. Rape was not the motive."

"The only thing I see here is hate," Jesse said. "Hate and anger."

Feinstein gave his two cents. "When we get the body downtown we'll know more of the specifics. But I tend to agree with Jesse."

Colefield wasn't done. He looked down at the taped off area and then back at the VA parking structure up the hill.

"It's close enough to where the Administrator was attacked. I don't think it's a coincidence. Christ, you can see the building from here. Someone from the group or someone from the hospital staff would have been privy that she was coming to the VA last night. They might have known she would be alone, and on foot, taking her usual path like she's done a dozen times before. Did you find a cell with her belongings?"

"No."

"Well, Harv," Colefield said. "As much as I'd like to stick around and help, I need to be down on Marine Drive if I want to keep the Lieutenant off my back. You'll let me know if something develops?"

Feinstein nodded and glanced over at Jesse whose face had turned to stone.

She said bluntly: "And you'll find me outside my sister's room with a .38 strapped to my ankle."

16

After dropping Jesse at the hospital, he headed north toward Marine Drive. Sunshine radiated on the green roof of the Sextant. Even after witnessing a brutal murder scene, Colefield couldn't drive by the landmark and not feel a tug at his heart strings. The urge to try again with Jill always raised its ugly head, even at the worst times, yet somehow this gave him a reason to go on, face the onslaught of violence … try and make a difference … take down the bad guys…

Just a couple hundred yards away from the Sextant, Colefield turned his pickup into the parking lot of the River Patrol Headquarters. Bart was the only one in the office when he walked in and flopped down behind his desk. Bart had a pair of binoculars and was looking at the daily parade down at the marina. Vehicles took turns backing trailers down the steep ramp to load boats. Bikini clad girls bounced about trying to help. Occasionally, arguments would erupt, and a few times they'd had to break up fights. Today everyone seemed to be getting along.

"Anything yet, Bart?"

"Nothing to report," he said. "I ran it by all the officers that responded to the accident. Nobody patrolling recalled seeing a Humvee or a Hummer that night. Boy — you gotta see these."

Colefield wasn't in the mood to check out the bikini crowd. He pulled his cell out of his pocket and laid it down on the desk, checked his email on the computer.

"Where's Weaver?"

"Hasn't made it in yet."

"And the Lieutenant?"

"Left ten minutes ago."

"Is Tony scheduled to come in?"

"He's pulling a shift down on the Willamette."

Bart lowered the binoculars, turned and faced him. "Wow! You look rough. You pull an all-nighter?"

"Feinstein called me to a murder up at the VA this morning. Might have something to do with Dr. Dafoe's accident. It was grim."

"Anything I can do?"

"You can start by topping off the tanks on the sled. And prepping the gear."

"Done and done."

Colefield got up, went into the locker room and changed into his uniform. When he returned to the office he picked up his Blackberry, slipped it into a case, and fastened it to his belt. Then he grabbed a handheld radio off the charger rack and strapped it to the front of his tactical vest. He checked his other gear, pulled his knife out of a lower drawer, and strapped it to the inside of his left ankle.

Bart looked over at him. "Aren't we waiting for Weaver?"

"I thought you and I would take a run to Lemon Island. See if anyone witnessed anything the other night. If Weaver gets here before we leave we'll take him along."

"Hey, I almost forgot. Harvey called."

"What'd he want?"

"Didn't say, said it was probably nothing."

"He say to call him back?"

"No rush, he said."

"Did the Lieutenant mention if the Incident officer from the other night filed his report?"

"Nope."

"You hear anything more on the VA administrator?"

"Her death popped up on Facebook. A few people commented but no leads ... how's the doctor doing?"

"Still in a coma. Print out the Facebook comments and put them on my desk. I'll be right back."

Colefield went out a side door into the garage. One of the boats was in for repair. The cover was off the outboard engine, parts lay scattered about a work bench.

Colefield opened his locker and it stank of river slime. Dirty, rank, uncleaned dive gear hung inside. The fins were covered in algae and reeds. Rather than rinsing the equipment off properly, he'd just stowed it the other morning, something he never did, and now regretted.

After he peeled off his tactical vest and slung it over the door, he carried the gear outside and hung it up. He found a hose and began to spray it off. The memory was still so clear — the tall willowy grass, the badly bruised face, her bare feet. There had been any number of places far easier and closer for her to have swum ashore, so why choose the reeds? Why up river against current? Why not the beach visible from the road? Was she trying to conceal herself? Or did the River Rat have something to do with this?

Colefield finished washing his gear, put on his tactical vest, shut off the lights, and went inside the office.

Bart was texting and looking restless, eager to get going. "Weaver's helping a stranded motorist on I-5. He'll be a while."

"Let's go. Grab your vest."

The river was choppy, not that uncommon in the summer. Bart loved it, saying it was like galloping on a big horse. By the time it funneled down the Columbia to Portland, gusts of around 25 knots were common, which the attendees of weekly yacht club races thrived on. As Bart piloted the boat upriver, Colefield counted a number of brightly colored spinnaker sails dotting the blue sky.

Sandwiched between Lemon Island on the western end and McGuire Island on the eastern end sat Government Island. Two channels separated the chain of islands. Commercial traffic mostly kept to the northern side because the southern side had plenty of shallows, sand bars, and deadheads sticking up near shore. Government Island was the largest, a big teardrop mass mostly flat with some steep embankments in the center. The beach hosted throngs of partiers and campers during the summer months because of their ease of access. The uncrowded channels also provided safe anchorages. Being an island chain, a boat or Jet Ski was needed to reach them. Some homeless had managed to float over on homemade rafts to build primitive camps in the more remote areas. They would stay as long as provisions, weather or the law allowed.

As a result, the islands could at times be a dangerous place...

The breeze whipped across Colefield's face, but his cap stayed on, pulled down snug over his sunburnt ears. His mind drifted to the accident scene again, as he looked far ahead toward shore. Bart's cellphone chirped and he handed off the helm to Colefield, moved to the forward chair and kept one eye on the river and the other on his cell phone. Bart stopped texting long enough to point out a sailboat up ahead that was tacking into their path and Colefield made a course adjustment to maneuver around it.

Lemon Island came into view first, a small spit of beach, vegetation, and a patch of oaks. The sun sliced through the tops of the trees and painted the sandy shoreline in a tangerine haze. Plenty of pleasure craft were anchored along the narrows on the northern side. Tents were set up along the beach and a few barbecues were smoldering. Three smaller crafts had tied off to the southern side near the point. From there, everybody had a view of the crash site. Colefield steered toward that area.

As land approached, Colefield killed the engine and glided the sled to shore away from the bonfires. Bart jumped off with the bow line and gave a little extra tug as the hull skidded to a stop in the deep sand. He tied off to an old stump and looked around.

Above them along the hillside, a couple of kids burst from the trees shouting and chasing each other down toward the water with pump-action squirt guns. Colefield climbed out and stood on the opposite side of the boat. He assumed the kids were part of a larger group camped out along the beach. Multicolored kites darted across the sky. Parents lounged in lawn chairs enjoying the scene. Somebody had built another fire pit further upriver. Kids were scouring for dried branches and wood. Others were off in their own camps, mostly just couples or small groups, drinking, sunbathing, and listening to music from boom-boxes. A few were making lazy attempts at packing it in for the day so they could leave before nightfall.

Colefield spotted a group of teenagers nearby. It looked by the sight of their campsite like they'd been there awhile. Stacks of wood by a deep fire pit, an impressive pyramid of beer with half as many empties piled up, a hefty tower of canned goods and plenty of fruit stowed under one end of a folding picnic table. Tents were old and sun-bleached, as were the folding tables and chairs. The equipment had seen plenty of hard use. There were two Jet Skis tied up at the water's edge along with a small powerboat and some wet inner-tubes.

When the deputies showed up, one of the guys dropped what looked like a joint on the ground by his bare feet, feigned indifference, and kicked a little sand over it just in case one of the deputy's was the wiser. The area reeked of pot.

Bart looked over at his partner waiting to see if he was going to jack the kid. Colefield had seen him drop the joint but wasn't concerned at the moment. Instead, he approached someone different, a lanky barefoot camper in surfer shorts polishing off a can of PBR. The kid had a scruffy in-charge look and didn't seem the least bit concerned about his sunburned chest.

As Colefield approached him, the kid crumpled up his aluminum beer can and tossed it behind him onto the stack. "Hey, boss man! What's up?"

"Just out keeping people safe. Been here long?"

"Since Friday. We're planning on staying through the fourth. It can get pretty crazy finding a good camping spot if you don't come early."

Colefield scanned the young faces. "You're all twenty-one, right?"

A guy and girl standing in the background with sand-sprinkled skin darted behind one of the tents.

"Yeah, sure. There's no problem here."

"What's your name?"

"Jack."

"What about the two hiding behind the tent?" Colefield asked. "Were they here the other night?"

"Yeah, sure."

"Hey, you two!" Colefield shouted. "Come out here!"

The two teens reluctantly stepped out into the open and showed themselves. The girl blushed, crossed her arms over her chest as if the rope bikini was exposing too much skin. Both of them looked a little drunk or high.

"Us?" the girl uttered.

"Just get over here."

The two wandered over, stood behind Jack, who tried to maintain his bravado, by standing between them and the officers. Everybody sort of shuffled in closer as a group.

"See anything unusual on the other side of the river Saturday night?" Bart asked them. "Say about 11:30 or so?"

For clarity, Colefield pointed out the area. A few heads turned and looked. No one was taking the lead, admitting anything.

Bart repeated the question. "So, nobody saw the accident?"

Jack shook his head and looked at the others. It was the gangly white kid who had been smoking the joint who started to say something and then changed his mind. He ran his hand through a pile of hair all twisted up into some glorious turban with rope and twine ribbons, picked a twig or something out of the mess and flicked it to the ground.

Colefield wasn't going to allow them to blow him off. "You over there — with the hair — got something you'd like to tell us?"

The kid rolled his head and shuffled around nervously. Bart moved in. "You heard my partner."

"Chill, dudes. I'll get there." The kid scratched the underside of each arm. "OK … OK … like it's late Saturday. Party has winded down. Everyone's racked out including me. I'm trying to enjoy a nice flat-line on some Double Bubble. The weed's awesome. My mind is tuning in to its rhythms, you know. Suddenly, I hear this loud ca-splash! I freak out a little. I can't make sense of it. Whole earth feels like it's shakin', you know? I jump out of my sleeping bag and look around. There's this ghost-like dude on the bike path across the river, shining a beam of light down at the water and he takes off running toward it. Then I see what he's looking at, this eruption — a volcano rumbling in the water. Man, it was spooky. The car just floats there, right — all that metal, man. Then, it just burps and takes a big nose dive down and gurgles out of sight. Then this dude like he's cat fast. He's like airborne. It was miracle ass shit."

"You're losing me, kid."

"Maybe it was the Double Bubble, maybe it was the shrooms, I don't know. It was out of this world, he like just dives into a rumbling volcano of water. I watch for a long time the light bouncing around under there. Then suddenly the light goes off and he shoots out of the water with this lady thrown over his shoulder and takes off."

"Takes off where exactly?"

"I don't know, man. When his light went off, I couldn't see shit after that."

"Did you see any other cars on the road?"

"Yeah, I saw another car. It stopped on the road over there." The kid pointed to an area just west of the crash site.

"Did the driver get out?"

The kid scratched his balls. "No. It just stops a sec then vanishes."

"How soon after the accident did this vehicle show up?"

"It didn't show up after, man. It was there all the time."

"You're confusing me. Did this vehicle have anything to do with the accident?"

"I don't know. It was just there."

Bart crossed his arms. "You're sure you weren't dropping acid?"

"Dude, this is for real. It was trippy but I wasn't trippin'…"

"We had a witness who reported it," Bart cut in. "Our witness arrived about ten minutes or so after the accident. You're sure you're not getting the two confused?"

The kid shook his head. "By the time that dude got there it was all over."

"What else do you remember?"

"She was like a dolphin, man. All wet and slick and scared shitless. And the dude just whisks her out of the water and rescues her."

Colefield looked the kid over closely. He didn't see any track marks on his arms. "And the car on the road, they didn't aid? They just drove away?"

"That's right."

Colefield softened his voice, tried a different approach. "What's your name, son?"

"Mitch, man. Mitch Steves."

"Think hard, Mr. Steves. This is very important. How many people did you see in the water?"

"The dude and the lady."

"You didn't think to go get help?" Bart asked.

"No time. The water stopped rumbling. The dude was gone. The lady was ashore. Everything went creepy quiet. I popped a gummy, and went out with the tide..."

17

The consensus from the other campers on Lemon and Government Islands was in. No one had seen shit. The best information had come from Mitch. Somewhere in his stoned tale was a nugget of truth. Colefield wasn't going to discount the kid's entire story as a drug induced fabrication. He needed more time to put the pieces together. If there was another vehicle at the scene — it meant someone out there was hiding something. They could have caused the accident or been privy to it. This gave credence to what the River Rat had told him. With the Air National Guard base on the southwest side of the airport, it also could have been a military vehicle on maneuvers.

Obviously, the rescuer was used to being around chaos and keeping a clear head, which was the take-away message. He suspected River Rat fit that bill. He felt frustrated he'd not been able to get more out of him. Why had he done it? He didn't want to be a hero, or he would have taken credit.

Maybe he believed in offering a 'do over', a second chance.

Colefield wasn't ready to call it a day. He thought about giving the wheelhouse to Bart but changed his mind at the last minute and told the young deputy to take point to McGuire Island. He found the right moment to tell him what he knew about the *Rat*. They would search the channel there for him. Maybe he lived on one of the islands or on a boat.

The wind had started to die down to 3 or 4 knots and the white caps cresting the river earlier were smoothing out with the waning tide. The river looked like the backside of an enormous sturgeon, its scaly tail prodding the surface, shivering with gray ripples.

Sagging oak and spruce hung out over the channel — crusty branches dangling with pockets of damp moss, Hobo spiders and swarms of mosquitos. Bart knocked a few limbs aside as the sled turned into a narrow channel. The area was heavily shaded with just a whisper of light to navigate by. The humid air was fertile with the scent of rotting wood and decaying vegetation. Dense reeds scraped the hull and had to be carefully maneuvered around to avoid fouling the prop.

"It's pretty shallow here. Just how far you want to push it?"

"We're still at six feet," Colefield told him. A gaggle of geese flew overhead. After their piercing cries faded, he heard other sounds. Creatures scurrying off through the brush — stray cats, rats, possums. And it had him on edge. The low hanging limbs, the restricted visibility, the fact that at any moment they could tangle a prop in a twist of reeds. He could barely see beyond the bow and turned on a spotlight.

Beyond where their light was shining — in fact much further — was an unmistakable turbine-like, whishing or whooshing noise. It was coming from the channel but where exactly? Somewhere out between the two islands.

"You hear that, Bart?"

"What the hell is it?"

"I'm asking you — farm boy. You're the expert."

"Beats the fuck out of me."

"Wait!" Colefield shouted. "Look to starboard, you see that?"

Colefield thought he saw movement — a dark object off in the distance, at the edge of a wooded area. Then it moved closer. It showed itself briefly and then vanished.

"Must have been a deer," he said.

"It didn't look like a deer. I don't know what the hell I saw."

Up ahead the channel narrowed to almost a pinpoint. Colefield glanced down at the depth meter and it read four feet. They still had clearance but barely. He'd try to push out to the other side if conditions allowed but vegetation choked each side of the bank and he had his doubts they would succeed.

"We're going to have to turn around. We can try again later at high tide."

"Hold up," Bart said.

Colefield dumped the transmission into neutral. The boat glided to a stop, idling quietly while Bart strained to catch sight of something along the shoreline. "Bart, what is it?"

"That strange noise? I don't hear it anymore."

They waited in silence for it to return.

Whatever they thought they'd seen or heard was gone.

* * *

Someone was manning the office when the deputies approached the Gleason Boat Ramp. Bart cleared the hull of dead branches, twigs and leaves, tossing the debris overboard into the current and then gathered up the lines and loose gear. They idled around to the boathouse and glided inside the dark barn. Colefield killed the engine.

Weaver met them down at the boathouse moments later. Supposedly he wanted to fill them in on a few of the calls that had come in while they were out at Government Island. It was a ruse. Weaver just wanted out of the office to stretch his sizeable legs and sneak in a smoke.

His uniform was wrinkled like he'd slept in it when he flipped on the overheads and walked over to the sled, a lit stogie in hand.

"That ranks right up there with one of those weird moments," Bart said, climbing out to tie off the bow line. Colefield tossed Weaver the stern line and then climbed out.

The two deputies were still processing it.

"We'll resume our little trip down the Amazon tomorrow when the tide's up and we have clearance. We'll try it again from the north side of the channel next time."

"You guys turn up something tonight?" Weaver stooped down and tied off.

It was as if the other deputy didn't exist. "That was fuckin' weird, Colefield."

"Let's drop it."

"Weaver crossed his arms and glared at them. "Drop what?"

"We'll tell you over a beer."

Weaver shook his head. "Not right now. We just got a distress call of a boat in trouble."

18

It was decided Colefield would man the office while Bart and Weaver headed back out. Colefield tossed his cap on the desk and then looked around to see if anyone had left any paperwork for him. A new "Missing Person" poster had been dropped off by the Sheriff's Department. He went over and pinned it up on the cork board.

He glanced out the window toward the marina and didn't see the sled moored at the end dock. Things were quiet on the water. There were still a few sunbathers lingering around on the warm night and several dogs running loose down by the river with their owners jogging behind.

Colefield changed out of his wet shirt and went through the usual checks of his gear and headed outside. He walked down to boathouse #2 and looked inside. The barn was empty. Evidently, Tony had taken a few of the summer cadets out in the 26-footer on a training exercise. Something he saw in a memo that came through his email. The 22-footer was still decommissioned in the shop. Becker hadn't made much progress on getting parts. Anymore when something broke down, parts were always on back-order.

He figured the Lieutenant was gone for the night. He'd probably taken the squad car. So Colefield stood on the dock and stared out at the river. There wasn't much of a breeze. Water was smooth as glass. Mt. St. Helens and Mt. Hood were gleaming in hazy sunset while Mt. Adams poked its snowy peak up through some fluffy clouds. It was in the lower 80's, a perfect summer night. Off in the distance a plane was making its approach to the runway from the east. He noticed a bright reflection on the glass of the airport tower.

It came back again in flashes, the wreckage on the river bottom, her broken body in the willowy reeds, the conversation with the stoner kid on Lemon Island.

A few seagulls flew by and landed on the telephone lines over by the Sextant. He was surprised he hadn't thought to look in the parking lot when he and Bart motored in off the river to see if Jill's car was there. He strained to see if he could catch a glimpse of the Subaru in the back lot. It wasn't there.

When he turned back around the red lights of the airport tower caught his eye.

Files with red dots ... wasn't that what Dr. Rosin had mentioned?

Red dots…

He heard the throaty sounds of a familiar outboard splashing toward the landing. He looked up in time to see the sled with a ski boat tied to its port side. Weaver was up on the bow, looking like a wet spaniel. Bart was manning the helm, while the teenage campers they had interviewed on Lemon Island: Jack, Jody and Bruce, huddled near each other. The only person not present was Mitch, the stoner.

He waited for Weaver to toss him the bow line, caught it on the first try, and draped it over the dock cleat before tying off the stern. Weaver got out first.

"What happened to them?" Colefield asked.

"Little engine trouble."

"The stoner kid's still out there," Bart said. "These guys said he took off. They don't know where he went. They were looking for him until the engine stalled."

Colefield reached out and helped Jody over the bow and onto the dock. She was sunburned from head to toe now. Her arms and legs were lobster claws. Weaver helped Bruce out. He'd twisted his ankle. Jack climbed over the stern refusing Bart's help.

They clung together on the dock like they were waiting for a beating. Three wet, tired, filthy, refugees smelling like sardines. Jack rocked his head around, cracking his neck a few times.

"So, where's Mitch?" Colefield asked Jack.

"He took off after you guys left."

Colefield looked at Jody. "Which way did he go?"

She turned and pointed toward Government Island.

"Why did he take off?"

"He wanted to find the guy from the other night."

"Great. So, Jack — is this your boat?"

Jack pointed to a shiny black Suburban with a boat trailer in the parking lot. "It's my dad's."

"Can you drive, OK?"

"Sure. I'm sober."

"You wouldn't be lying, would you? I can break out the breathalyzer."

"He's telling you the truth," Bruce said. "He hasn't had a drop since you guys spoke with us."

"What about Mitch?" Jody jumped on the defensive suddenly.

"Let us worry about him."

"He's got the Jet Ski."

Bart stared at Colefield.

"Jody — does Mitch live at home or does he have his own place?" Colefield asked.

"He lives at home."

"Give me his parent's number."

Jody patted down the pockets of her white cutoffs twice. "Oh, man. I lost my phone. Jack, do you have it?"

"Why would I have it?"

"Bruce?"

"You had it on the beach."

"Shit, shit, shit."

Colefield lost his patience. "Just give me their names."

Jody turned and leaned over and pawed around inside Jack's boat.

"Just give me their names," Colefield repeated. "I can get the number later."

"Micki and Mike Steves. And he's got two younger sisters — Marge and Monica. They're known as the 'M&M' family."

"Cute. What about an address?"

"They used to live in Vancouver on Z Street. But they moved recently. I don't know where."

19

The following morning, Colefield was back at his desk bright and early, cradling a steaming cup of very strong coffee back. He'd just gotten off the phone with a sleepy-voiced Jesse. She'd been at the hospital late and hadn't slept well. There was still no improvement in her sister's condition. He checked in with Feinstein but got his voicemail.

Bart rolled in ten minutes later, his hair still wet from the shower. Tony and Weaver let Colefield know they were taking the cruiser to follow-up on a break-in at Jantzen Beach Marina. The office had that familiar bustling feel to it. Phones were ringing, the marine radio was squawking, Colefield wanted to speak with the deputies before they left but answered one of the phones instead. The caller wanted to know about fishing restrictions and Colefield directed them to the Fish and Wildlife Division and hung up. The Lieutenant was in his usual cheery mood, barking at someone on his private office phone. His loud voice carried to the outer office while the smell of fresh donuts filled the air.

A box of Voodoo Donuts rested on the breakroom table. Colefield walked by it and was tempted but resisted the sugar buzz, and instead topped off his coffee.

Bart walked up and grabbed a big chocolate donut and shoved it into his mouth and chomped away.

In a garbled voice, Bart said: "Beats oatmeal."

"Don't choke. I need you today. We're going to take a run out to Harbinger Cove."

"Where the hell is that?"

"East of where we called it quits last night. I thought we'd make another pass by the islands to see if the kid has returned to camp and then take a run upriver, see if we can't find the *Rat*."

"I better grab another donut … might be a while before we get lunch."

The light was uplifting and refreshing, the air already very warm. It was going to be another scorcher; KGW was predicting 103 degrees by five o'clock. It'd be a busy one on the river.

They made a quick pass by the island. After no sign of the kid they headed east. When they finally reached Harbinger Cove, Bart had to steer the boat in a generally easterly direction to avoid the tall reeds off the starboard bow. The river was rippling from a breeze that had kicked up suddenly. Bart threw some throttle at the current running against them. A flock of geese took flight as their boat grew nearer to land. Bart eased back on the throttle and steered into a fertile cove surrounded by trees, scrub brush and rotting logs. The area was protected from the elements. They didn't see a Jet Ski. But about twenty-five feet from the river bank, they floated up on a derelict flotilla.

It was ingenious, Colefield thought. Made from three makeshift rafts — a collection of wooden pallets roped together floating on barrels — a motor-less open bow dinghy and a sailboat with a tattered main luffing in the wind with an unfurled jib tied off to one of the stanchions. One of the rafts had what looked like two electric outboard motors mounted to the back. The dinghy tied to it was filled with old computer and electronic equipment and plastic crates with an assortment of repair manuals, worn paperbacks and old magazines. Another raft had a bank of solar panels erected with battery cables attached to a dozen or more batteries and various hand tools and disassembled small motors piled up. The third raft had a large blue tarp erected over it. Two 55-gallon plastic barrels sat upright with a sheet of lumber over the top creating a workbench of sorts with a vice attached along with some hand tools. The area in front of it was filled with what looked like miscellaneous bicycle parts and scrap metal. The sailboat was also a piece of work. It looked as if it hadn't been drydocked in years. Had nicks and scrapes along its hull and teak trim sun-bleached with age and algae. A wind generator attached to the stern on the port side wobbled precariously as its prop rotated. Opposite it was a rusted barbecue with a bag of charcoal spilt into the cockpit area. Two solar panels rigged amid-ship, opened back like clam shells, collecting the last of the day's solar rays. Deck-side was littered with various antennas, plastic gallon jugs of what looked like used motor oil, ice chests, fishing poles, tackle, old ammo boxes, rope, gasoline cans, wooden and plastic paddles, life jackets, and a boom box.

Colefield made special note of the boat's name painted on the stern: *"Second Chance."*

The river patrol boat circled the flotilla, checking it over carefully before drawing closer. He kept a hand near his Glock and shouted out: "Multnomah County River Patrol! If anyone is aboard, come out! We'd like a word!"

Their boat glided to a stop rearward of the sailboat. He kept his eye focused on the hatch. They waited and then after no response Colefield shouted again.

He relaxed his grip on his weapon. "Didn't we see this same vessel over by Cathedral Park last winter?"

"We may have."

"Tags are current. Let's run the numbers."

Bart called the office on the two-way. The Lieutenant answered and Bart read off the registration numbers and asked for a routine registration check. After a few minutes, a loud voice came back on the radio.

Colefield listened in: "Boat is registered to a corporation called Womack Machine Industries. Their address is listed as

11515 N Marine Drive. The boat in question is a 26-foot San Juan built in 1983. They are the original owners. No report of it being stolen. And where the hell are Tony and Weaver? I need my cruiser."

Colefield grabbed the microphone. "We're going to hang and see if anyone shows up here. Did Weaver brief you on the kid from last night?"

"He mentioned it. Where are all the cadets?"

"Red Cross training, sir."

"Figures." The radio went dead.

Colefield hung up the microphone and looked around. Except for a pair of mallards splashing around in the water near shore, the rest of the area was quiet. Colefield figured there should be some bird chatter somewhere, especially this early. He felt a little prickle along his neckline and had a familiar feeling they were being watched.

"Keep alert, Bart. Something doesn't feel right."

Their boat circled the flotilla a second time, checking it over carefully. The hatch remained closed. Colefield didn't see a padlock. The wind generator was spinning freely making the now familiar whishing sound they had heard earlier. It heightened the eerie sense hanging over the place.

Colefield glanced toward land. Even with the sunlight, thick vegetation and trees made it next to impossible to see clearly on the hillside. The boat idled toward land. "Kill the engine," Colefield said, taking a second look along the shoreline. Tracks were visible in the sand. A long groove that widened as it trailed into the vegetation line. It could only mean one thing.

"Let's get out."

Bart climbed out first and pulled the bow ashore. Colefield was right behind him.

"Stay with the sled, Bart."

The marks he had seen from the water were much easier to identify on land. They were fresh, still damp.

In the foliage ahead, Colefield bumped something with his boot. The forest green kayak had been pulled a few yards into the grass, out of sight.

To his right a trail led into the woods. Limbs, dried branches, overgrown vegetation, maneuvering through it all was very tedious. Colefield followed the path as best he could. The canopy of trees blocked out most traces of sunlight. An array of scents wrestled with his sinuses: musk and grass pollen and the odor of wet bark. Every sound amplified, especially his clothing snagging every low-lying branch and wild plant.

He stepped deeper into the thicket before resting by a cottonwood.

He heard a twig snap and turned. Out of the shade, a rugged man appeared from the backside of a tree. He was shirtless, his skin streaked in mud, his chest and arms covered in scratches. He had on worn khaki shorts. His military-issue boots bore broken and retied laces. There was a faded leather pouch tied around one side of his waist and a large bowie knife strapped to the other. Colefield kept his distance.

He felt the weight of intense eyes sizing him up. The man had unearthed an old footlocker near the tree.

"Hello Deputy Colefield." the man's voice was deep, gravelly, as if it were the first words he'd spoken in days.

"Nice seeing you again, *Rat*. Are you the owner of the San Juan in the cove?"

"You know I am."

"And your name would be?"

"Do we have to do this?"

"Unless, you'd prefer another way."

"Richard Raulings, Sergeant USMC, Last 4, 8763."

"What's in the footlocker?"

"Newspapers."

"Bring it or leave it. We need to have a discussion."

Raulings effortlessly hefted the footlocker onto his shoulder and marched ahead on the fresh path at a brisk pace, dodging branches and nettles like they didn't exist. Colefield used to walk that way, as a young man in the Navy. Every move done with purpose, every action thought out in advance.

When they reached the shoreline, Colefield called out. "Stop and drop the footlocker. Now remove your knife and leather pouch."

Bart hustled over. Raulings plopped the footlocker on the ground and began to remove the leather pouch. Colefield assumed surrendering the knife would not be an easy decision for him. Yet, he followed instructions, dropped the items and stepped back, calmly studying Colefield.

"Anything in your pockets?"

"Yes."

"Empty them."

The man dumped his front pockets and several round stones fell to the ground. Colefield figured there was something special about them. Bart kicked the knife out of reach. Next the man reached into his back pocket and removed a worn field notebook. He tossed it to the ground. Colefield eyed the notebook but left it and began to untie the leather pouch.

It didn't contain contraband. Instead it held herbs, bark chips and wild berries.

"What's this stuff?" Colefield asked.

"There are no McDonalds out here."

He returned the leather pouch. Colefield picked up the man's field book, flipped through a few pages. The writing was hard to read in the glare of the sun but seemed precise, filled with coordinates, way points, drawings of the surrounding islands, notes about food, vegetation and wildlife. He handed it back.

"Let's talk about the accident along Marine Drive."

Raulings turned his broad chin skyward, like he was reflecting. "The driver was unconscious. I got her to the surface. She took in some water but was breathing by the time I reached shore. I placed her in some tall grass and waited."

"Waited for what?" Colefield asked.

"To see if the driver of the Hummer intended to kill her."

"Did he come toward you?"

"No, but he saw me."

"Then he just took off? Was the wreck intentional?"

"Yes. He rammed her bumper, pushed her off the road into the river."

"Why'd you take off?"

"I didn't want to leave her alone. But I wanted to catch him before he left."

"On foot?"

"I thought he would stay longer."

"What about the license plate?"

"I told you before, I didn't see it."

"You're staying it was a newer model Hummer not a Humvee, right?"

"It was a tan Hummer."

"You're positive about the color?"

"Baby-shit brown, positive."

"Was there anyone with him?"

Raulings shook his head, started to speak and then stopped. Colefield studied him for a moment.

"There was nothing to hunt that night. The birds knew something was about to happen." Raulings paused. "You wouldn't know by looking but this island is filled with endangered species. They know how to survive without detection. They have been doing it for decades."

Colefield changed tactics. "Did you know her?"

"She looked different that night."

"Were you a patient of hers?"

"I had no idea it was Dr. Dafoe until I pulled her from the car."

Colefield probed. "What happened? Why'd you stop going to the VA?"

"I had my reasons."

Bart interrupted. "Where were you on the night of June 25th?"

"What happened on the night of June 25th?"

Colefield said, "A VA administrator was assaulted."

Raulings remained silent.

"What about two nights ago — between the hours of eight and ten — where were you?"

"Can I retrieve my knife now?"

"Leave it. We have reason to believe a soldier from Ms. Dafoe's group was murdered then. Her name was Zoey Elliot. Ring a bell?"

Colefield studied Rauling's face for any reaction. He didn't flinch, didn't move a muscle.

"Your flotilla looks packed and ready to go," Bart said. "Are you leaving?"

"You're jacking up the wrong guy, deputies," he said. "Find the Hummer and you'll find your killer."

Raulings drifted as if he was reliving some painful memory. Colefield recognized the look.

"Soldier! Can we continue?" Colefield barked.

Raulings snapped out of it. "I have something to show you."

Raulings opened the footlocker and began rummaging through the smelly stacks of newsprint. Colefield put his hand up to hold Bart back.

Raulings found something. He stood and handed a section of an old newspaper to Colefield.

"That's your guy," he said.

"What makes you so certain?"

"Just do your homework … or have Montgomery do it for you."

Colefield flinched. "You're …" *Of course, he was.* "How's the "limp dick" working out?"

"It's in a safe place. Nice old Ford you have. You should wash it."

"What's with the old newspapers?"

"They're obituaries of fallen soldiers. I collect them so I'll never forget."

Colefield was not holding an obituary. It was a sport's page, a full-spread front-page article with a photograph of a football player, who a few years back had the world by the balls until his fall from grace. Raulings, he figured, had the player's image lodged in his memory and it all came rushing back when he saw him at the crash site. Once he started putting it together, he knew where to look for the final missing piece.

"Read it aloud so your frisky deputy can hear."

Colefield looked at Bart. "It was a few years ago. Maybe you remember it, too — the Heisman Trophy hopeful with an older brother serving a second tour in Afghanistan? He was a key suspect in the mysterious death of a freshman girl at a frat party before the charges got dropped."

Colefield felt his stomach knot. A few days earlier, he'd bumped into Christian Riker at the VA and hadn't made the connection. He was still a tough-looking SOB — a little rougher around the edges now, a little more filled out. Dr. Rosin had said he had been angry because the VA administrator cut off his brother's funding.

Colefield looked Raulings in the eye. "I'll need your statement. I want you to come with us."

"I need to end this. I owe it to the others."

"What you owe is your cooperation and testimony to the DA."

Raulings nodded and looked like he was going to cooperate. Colefield let down his guard. The deputies turned, distracted long enough for Raulings to snatch up his knife and dart into the thick brush. It may have been futile in Colefield's mind but Bart drew his weapon and shouted. "Raulings! Freeze!"

It was a rookie move. Colefield ordered him to stand down. Bart holstered his weapon and then darted into the woods after him.

Bart pursued Raulings until his legs gave out. He was somewhere long gone or hiding so well they'd never find him. Perhaps he had another boat stashed somewhere on the island and was already on his way to God knows where.

When Colefield caught up to Bart, he was bent over, clutching his knees, gasping for air. His black uniform looked like the skin of a porcupine, covered in brown thistles and fluffy fragments of cattail.

"You get an A for effort," Colefield said. "And an F for not fucking thinking. What were you going to do? Fight him? Shoot him? He'd have torn you a new asshole with that buck knife."

"What was I supposed to do? Just let him get away?"

20

For the hundredth time Colefield surveyed the rim of the cove and surrounding woods. "Bart, hand me the binoculars again."

Bart turned them over. "Have you seen any good movies lately?" he asked out of the blue, clearly bored with the surveillance.

Colefield was focusing, not listening. "You see anything along the ridge?

"I could see better with binoculars."

"Funny guy."

Colefield raised his hand and gestured toward some bushes next to a very large tree along the outer ridge. Bart stared in the general vicinity.

"So, have you?"

"Have I what?"

"Seen any good movies lately."

"No."

"You think Betty is into chick flicks or action films?"

"Did you hear me?" Colefield asked.

"Yeah, yeah. I don't see anything."

"Are we talking Betty from the Sextant?"

"Her real name is Beatrice."

"Why don't you ask her opinion? You aren't sixteen, Bart."

"Maybe I'll check out what's playing at the Living Room Theater tomorrow. That's kind of a cool place, right? Have you been there?"

"Remember, we begin 12-hour shifts tomorrow."

A noise out on the river distracted them both.

Bart slapped his shoulder. "Sarge! Behind you!"

Colefield spun around in time to see a Jet Ski zip by out on the river. The rider was the right age, no life jacket, no shirt, just shorts, barefoot, wild hair blowing back in the wind, and hauling ass in the opposite direction. *Mitch!*

"Fire up the engine!"

"What about Raulings?"

"He isn't going far."

Colefield caught sight of the Jet Ski. The river patrol boat blasted past Government Island slowly gaining ground.

As Colefield gripped the railing, the grim reaper popped into his head. What triggered it was a small flag tied to an antenna on Rauling's flotilla because Montgomery had one just like it, blowing in the wind atop his houseboat's flagpole, right underneath the American flag.

The reaper, this universal symbol for an elite member of the Special Forces, was both a badge of honor and a reminder of the sword of death.

The night Nicole Dafoe launched her car off Marine Drive the reaper spared her. But had she been spared? And why later had it taken the innocent woman's life across the hall from her? Or the life of an innocent soldier she was trying to help?

He felt the wet breeze tumble across his bare cheeks and rush past his ears. The boat sliced through the current making good headway. As they drew closer to the Jet Ski, a fountain of water rose behind it, cascaded down in their path.

After telling Montgomery what he had seen the night of Nicole's accident, it stayed at the back of his mind festering. *What causes a mind to snap?*

Was it a lone neuron careening off its electrical highway, plunging into gray matter, or a sudden explosion of a synapse, the bridge that kept it all together? Or was it the daily onslaught of minutia and when the future seemed just another unavoidable, inescapable road to hell — this grim reaper inside a person's head?

All the fallen soldiers Raulings had cared about. Harboring this large collection of the grim reaper's work must have been his way to cope.

Lemon Island burst into view as the Jet Ski made a sudden turn and veered straight toward land. Colefield glanced at Bart and saw the excitement gleaming in his youthful eyes. This is what the younger deputy lived for. What every cop lived for, the chase, the adrenaline rush.

And in that split second, the stoner kid must have had a moment of insight, too. Because he cut the throttle and propelled the Jet Ski up like a surfer riding a cresting wave, extinguishing its forward momentum as he tumbled ashore.

Bart drove the patrol boat up on the beach skidding to a stop. The kid took off running for the trees. Colefield jumped off the bow in pursuit.

Colefield caught up with him on a ridge a few hundred yards from shore and tackled the shirtless teenager as if he'd sacked a linebacker at the one yard line. He cuffed him, pulled him to his feet, and began to read him his rights.

"What the hell were you thinking taking off like that?" Colefield uttered.

Mitch's face speckled with sand resembled an African mask. "I saw him."

"Saw who?"

"The super hero."

A half-hour later, an ambulance was waiting for them at the marina when the deputies arrived with Mitch in cuffs. He was still spun up. Could have been adrenaline, dope, a mental condition, or all the above. Colefield had made the call on the marine radio. It was time for a psych evaluation. He also had a few scrapes and cuts that needed tending. The paramedic who strapped him to the gurney assessed him on the spot, nodded at Colefield. Colefield stepped back while the man gave Mitch an injection that transformed him from a jacked-up teenager into a comatose bag of bones.

The miracle of narcotics…

After the ambulance left, Colefield and Bart headed into the office, dragging their tired butts to their desks. Weaver handed Colefield a report that had been messengered over. After a cursory reading, Colefield picked up his cell and dialed a familiar number.

"I need your help, Montgomery."

21

Montgomery scrolled down through the report that the security guard from the Port had delivered to Colefield.

After a long moment, he turned with a frown and handed it back to Colefield.

"Well?"

"Where'd you get this?"

"It doesn't matter. Just give me your opinion."

"You know I tell you this in strictest confidence. Sergeant Richard Raulings is a God damned hero in my book. Whatever else this report indicates, they left out all the meat. Someone has obviously redacted some salient facts. I know another version of it. Back in 2012, a Force Recon team of Marines were dropped down into Falluja on a covert mission. The mission had been compromised and they were ambushed. It was an eight-man team on the ground. Four were shot, two killed instantly, the others were injured. They lay in the open, locked down in a triangle of fire, and it would only be a matter of time before their ammo ran out and the big black curtain descended on all of them. One soldier — the man in this report — was already injured. He did something so damn fearless it negates my bravest moments in the trenches. Injured, he crawled behind the line of fire and took out every one of the bastards with a buck knife. Hand to hand. The purest form of killing there is. Because of his efforts only two soldiers died that day. And for his reward, the entire operation was erased from the big box in the sky. No medals, no accolades, no honors."

"Why?"

"It was black ops standard operating procedure. Deny all parties involved. No official record — at least none your average citizen will ever be able to verify. Damn shame if you ask me. Had to cover up a few of those in my day and I still lose sleep over it." Montgomery coughed. "Let's change the subject — shall we old boy?" He stood up from the table. "I'm off to my workstation because I've fallen behind schedule on the reloads. You want to be a sport and grab us lunch? And they'll be rum in it for you later if you take the garbage out."

"I'm already running late for a meeting. You're on your own. We'll talk later."

Colefield started to get up but sat back a moment. He watched Montgomery hobble upstairs, cane in hand, his breathing labored. And it hit Colefield like a sou'wester. This could be him in the future: old, cranky, womanless and alone.

Was this how he wanted to end up? He was certainly headed in that direction unless he made a change.

He felt a little unsteady as he stood up. He grabbed the garbage bag from the galley and was about to leave when something zipped by on the river. He walked over to the back door to take a closer look, but the person, the boat, or whatever it had been, was nowhere in sight. He turned back around and shouted upstairs.

"I owe you, Bill!"

Montgomery shouted from above. "You owe it to our spritely new neighbor to track down the bastard who dishonored her."

22

The weekly joint meeting between the deputies of the Willamette and Columbia River Patrol Headquarters began sharply at 1:30 at Norma's Kitchen.

Colefield was running late because of his talk with Montgomery and phoned Bart that he and Weaver could meet him there. They traveled down the channel and arrived in the sled a few minutes before he did. While tying off to the dock, Sergeant Blackstone, a female deputy, zipped in on a Jet Ski with Tony riding bitch. Deputy Duncan and Shell pulled into the parking lot in a cruiser and parked next to Colefield's pickup.

As half the team climbed the ramp toward the Cajun restaurant, Deputy Mansfield blasted in on a police model Kawasaki KZ1000, which he parked in front of the small building that overlooked the water.

Inside, the deputies found a long table that faced the windows that could accommodate them. There were several other customers sitting at stools that looked down on the Jantzen Beach moorage. The owner waved. He was a native of New Orleans where he got his start in the business before opening this quaint gem. He drove a classic convertible parked out front. He greeted them and handed out menus. He had a female helper today behind the counter who was frying up what smelled like catfish for the other gentlemen.

The deputies chitchatted a few minutes before placing their orders. Colefield told Bart to order him Gumbo and went to use the bathroom. When he returned, the deputies were listening to a dispatch that came through on Tony's handheld radio. Something about a robbery in progress but in a different county and the deputies didn't need to respond.

Colefield sat down and began the discussion.

"Tony, what's the status of the homeless camps along the Willamette right now?"

"Portland PD made a sweep under the Fremont Bridge and along the East Central side last week, which just flushed them further East. We've still got the issues with the camps located between the Railroad Bridge and all the way to the St John's Bridge."

"How many?"

"Thirty-eight at last count."

"What about the Columbia Slough area?"

"We've seen a reduction there, nine at last count. Duncan can tell you more. He responded to a domestic violence assault call there last Monday."

Duncan nodded. "I counted eight encampments while I was there. We hauled off one of the campers because he sliced up his wife's arm with the lid from a tuna can."

"Shell, what about the transient boats around Ross Island?"

"They're still a problem. The numbers are down to maybe 40 to 45. Residents and day visitors make complaints daily. They're bitching about the harm to wildlife habitat. We still have issues with litter and illegal waste dumping. A few of the engines are leaking oil into the river. Mostly, people just feel that since the no-wake zone came into effect, they've seen an increase in homeless flotillas and aging sailboats. They feel they're being taken over by scum and partiers."

"Copy that," Sergeant Blackstone said. "We have six living downriver, north of the Fremont Bridge. DEQ found PCB contaminants in the area. Some of the boaters are using the water for cooking and drinking despite the advisory against it."

"How'd the sweeps go on Government Island? I heard you, Tony and Shell made two outstanding warrant arrests?"

"Yeah, one of them hit Shell with a chain."

Shell held up his right hand and showed off his fresh stitches. "It's cut down on my masturbation," he joked.

"I think you'd have to amputate both of Tony's hands to get him to stop," Weaver said with a smile.

"Really, guys," Sergeant Blackstone said. "Enough with the juvenile antics."

Colefield jumped in. "We're trying to keep Dr. Nicole Dafoe's name out of the paper. I can't confirm it yet, but we believe there was another vehicle involved, somebody possibly wanting to kill her. We'll take another sweep of McGuire Island later today. There's a transient holed up there on a flotilla that may be our key witness. We spoke to him earlier and spooked him off. He gave us a possible suspect but I don't know if I can trust him or not. I wanted to give you a briefing on him and get a better picture of what the transient populations are, both in our area and yours in case I need to look elsewhere to flush him out. I may have to bring some of you in for backup. When we did a pass of McGuire Island earlier, it was only him on hook. For all I know he could have recruited some others to keep us away or moved. He could be anywhere."

Bart spoke up. "Don't want to spoil the fun, but the food's coming."

Colefield spun around as the owner began dumping plates of catfish and pulled pork around the table. His helper was refilling water glasses.

After they had gone, Colefield resumed. "On the surface this guy fits the mold of a survivalist: Big flotilla, weathered sailboat, dinghies, kayak, 55-gallon drums of scrap metal and electronic parts, and dozens of outboards. You get the picture."

"Sounds like Munsen's flotilla near the Slough," Duncan said.

"Or Peterson's near Sauvie Island."

Colefield took a bite of gumbo, pulled a shrimp tail out of his mouth and set it down on a napkin. "I believe his name is Richard Raulings. He's ex-military, highly specialized, Force Recon. He's a combat vet and highly talented with weaponry and extremely self-reliant. He lives off birds and animals he hunts and kills. What his mental health is like or if he has a grudge against law enforcement is still unclear. Have any of you had dealings with him before?"

The table fell quiet with a consensus of head shaking.

"I can check with Columbia County," Blackstone said. "I know a guy there. See if they've had any contact with him in their waters. Hey, Shell, didn't you say your brother works as a nurse at the VA. Maybe he's heard of the guy."

Shell slid back his chair and pulled out his cell. "Let me see if I can reach him."

Blackstone did the same for her contact.

Colefield turned and looked out the window. Down on the dock, a father and son were checking out the River Patrol boat. He turned back around when Shell got off his cell.

"Negative," Shell said.

"Double negative," Blackstone added. "Have you tried any of the outreach groups or homeless advocates?"

"They're dealing with roughly 4000 homeless right now and they're stretched pretty thin. One on one is pretty rare. I called *Street Roots*, got the editor on the line. Helpful in general but didn't have any personal knowledge of Raulings."

"What about the editor of *The Fishing News*?" Duncan said. "What's his name? He published that good article last year on river dwellers. A reporter came out and interviewed us. Tony — what's the guy's name?"

Tony had a mouthful of collard greens. "I don't remember."

"I'll wrap this up. Most of you know Detective Feinstein. He called me out to a grizzly homicide that occurred in the woods surrounding the VA. A young female beaten to death — a combat vet. We don't know if there's a connection. We do know that the victim was one of Dr. Dafoe's patients."

Weaver put his cell away and shook his head.

"We'll see what we find at the flotilla again." Colefield chugged his glass of water. He stood and pulled out his wallet. His cell rang. He looked at the caller ID. "I've got to take this," he said and headed toward the door.

Outside, the bright sunlight was harsh. "Dr. Rosin, thanks for calling me back so soon."

"My God it's been a disheartening time around the VA. With the VA administrator, then the doctor, and now one of her patients — it feels like we need to do what we did at Sing Sing during a crisis — go into lockdown."

"Were you able to dig up anything on Richard Raulings?"

"I got your message. I'm looking down at his file here on my desk. One second," she said, and then used a Kleenex to blow her nose. "Sorry about that. Your hunch was correct. He was indeed a patient of Nicole's. Her notes are rather encrypted, but she was seeing him for PTSD and depression. He has tinnitus probably from his combat experience. I see he was her first client. She saw him on four occasions. Then his treatment stopped. There's no indication why. Before that, I see that he checked into the VA several times following his discharge in 2012. Then there appears to be a long gap in treatment until he recently resumed again with Dr. Dafoe."

"Is there anything about Raulings that would indicate he had a grudge against Dr. Dafoe or any of the other vets?"

"It's unclear," she said. "I see that he's described as a loner. He's experienced paranoia, bouts of depression and reportedly has had several angry outbursts toward other veterans. He was kicked out of the Vancouver VA for threatening behavior. Classic PTSD. And the bouts of anger toward other veterans — not out of the ordinary, really. They themselves stop seeking treatment because they're afraid they're going to hurt someone. And, I see here, he is homeless. This could be aggravating his condition. There's no indication he's self-medicating with alcohol or other drugs, which sets him apart from the rest of the group. Clearly, Dr. Dafoe took an interest in him. But I would consider him unstable."

"Was he ever a member of the group?"

"Let me take a look … wait … interesting."

"What did you find?"

"Looks like in the beginning Raulings attended several of the group sessions. He probably knows Zoey Elliot and the others."

"He admitted as much to me but I wanted to follow-up with you."

"Not him, not another veteran."

"I'm not sold that he's our killer. In fact, quite the opposite."

"How are you doing with all this, Jason? I must admit, I looked into your records as well. Your tours of duty were no picnic."

"No ma'am."

"Is this having a reactionary response with you?"

"If you mean, has it cause me some PTSD, yes. But I've got a handle on it."

"You deserve to give yourself a break."

"I will once I'm done with all this."

"It could be too late then."

That struck a strong cord in him. There was a pause on the line. Rosin, he figured, was letting her comment sink in or making some notes or both.

"Any change in Nicole's condition?" she finally asked.

"I'm afraid not."

"If anyone deserves another shot, she does."

23

Colefield felt off. He told Bart and Weaver he'd meet them back at the office. He had a few other stops to make first.

He picked up Jesse at her hotel, tried to hide the anxiety he was feeling while they headed out to the North Precinct Impound Yard. The yard, surrounded by a metal fence and topped with serpentine wire, was located near the Burlington Northern railroad tracks off Marine Drive. Colefield had visited the place a number of times, mostly when he was involved in vehicle recovery, and he always had the families of the victims to think about. They needed to grieve, to comfort a loved one, while crying over the wreckage. Their live forever altered. Never the same, never another opportunity to say: "I'm sorry or I love you." No second chances for what went unsaid and undone.

Set back off the road, against a backdrop of tall trees and old warehouses, the place doubled as a wrecking yard. Several hundred old cars in various stages of rust and disrepair littered one side of the lot. The other side held vehicles in better shape. Near the back was a separate storage area for abandoned vehicles and equipment that for one reason or another had been impounded. Colefield stared out at old power boats, worn-out tractors, school buses with blacked out windows and wondered what the backstory was on them. A dozen or more wrecked vehicles sat in front by the entrance. Colefield didn't see the Mercedes among them. Jesse was adamant about inspecting her sister's vehicle personally. And Colefield was preparing himself for another heartbreak.

The gate was open. He drove through and parked beside a dilapidated double-wide trailer, the only physical structure he saw on site.

An equipment operator in greasy coveralls climbed off a forklift near the building and charged through the door just ahead of them.

He was disheveled and sweaty with gray stubble streaking his ruddy face. He pushed his cap back on his head and stepped behind a long counter, walked to a time clock and punched his timecard. A middle-aged woman nibbling on what looked like a baloney sandwich slipped her slender hand inside a small bag of potato chips open on the counter. She tossed a chip in her mouth, then set the sandwich down, picked up a napkin and wiped a smear of mayonnaise from her chin.

"What can I do for you two?" she asked, while the man helped himself to the bag of chips. "Johnny! Out of those!"

The equipment operator grinned. He swiped salt from his lips, bent over and whispered something into the woman's ear while he grabbed his thermos from under the counter.

"I'm deputy Colefield with the River Patrol, this is —"

Before he could finish the sentence, Jesse spoke up, meeting the woman's gaze. "I'm Jesse Dafoe. I understand my sister's Mercedes is here."

"What's the name?"

"Dafoe. Nicole Dafoe."

"When did the vehicle come in?"

"The 30th," Colefield said.

"June?"

"June," Jesse replied, taking a dislike to the woman immediately. "We didn't see it near the gate."

"That's cuz it's not there. That area is reserved for vehicles held for auction."

The woman glanced down at her sandwich and sighed. She spun around on her chair turning her back to them and dug through a stack of papers. There was a computer terminal on the counter but she ignored it.

"It's a police impound," Colefield said.

"Most of 'em are."

"She was involved in an accident, if that helps," Jesse added.

"What was the name again?"

"Nicole Dafoe."

"And you say you're the sister?"

"That's right," Jesse said, moving about the office, looking it over like a state health inspector, running her finger along the edge of the counter. By the frown on her lips, this place did not meet her standards.

Jesse turned and said. "We can wander the yard ourselves. Just point us in the right direction and we'll be out of your hair."

"Afraid I can't allow that. I gotta verify paperwork first."

"Well, honey, if you want me to help. Just slide a stack my way and I'll dig through it myself."

"What's the name on the vehicle again?" the woman asked, ignoring Jesse's comment.

Colefield jumped in. "Dafoe. Nicole Dafoe. Perhaps it's listed under Dr. Nicole Dafoe."

The woman mouthed the words back. "Dah Foe? Spell it for me."

Colefield felt the urge to strangle her. Instead, he took a deep breath, let it out slowly, waiting for the flash of anger to subside. "D-A-F-O-E."

The woman was oblivious to his near outburst. "Well, I don't see it in this stack. I guess there is another place it could be," she moved back from the desk, walked to the end of the counter, reached underneath and removed a different stack of papers. She dropped them down on the countertop with a thud, began sorting, one page at a time. Eventually, she reached the middle of the stack and something caught her eye.

"Here it is ... yeah, the vehicle came in on the 30th like you said. I couldn't find it because the vehicle has California plates. All out-of-state vehicles get filed separately."

"How orderly," Jesse said sarcastically.

The clerk read the document very slowly. "The vehicle is in area C, row C, space 13. She pointed out the window. If you go back out the door and turn left, follow the driveway down to Area C, you'll see our markers. If you need any help, Johnny should be wandering around. He might be on a coffee break though."

The two started toward the exit.

"Hold up! You'll need to sign our guest log before I can allow you into the yard."

She nodded toward a clipboard with a yellow pad and pen on a chain by the computer terminal. Colefield grabbed it, scribbled something down on the tablet and put it back.

"I'll need both signatures on it," the woman picked up her partially eaten sandwich and stared at Jesse. Jesse brushed past Colefield and signed the sheet of paper.

Walking across the gravel yard, Colefield glanced up at the crude wooden pole markers the woman had mentioned. Just three more rows to go. They continued walking. Up ahead, Colefield spotted it. The convertible looked different in the bright sunlight. It might have been the way the light reflected off the shattered windshield.

Jesse froze and gasped. "My god..."

Colefield left her there and circled the car several times, examining it up close. Jesse came over eventually and stood by the driver's side door peering inside the vehicle.

The key in the ignition had a rabbit's foot dangling from it. Broken glass cluttered the floorboard and littered both seats. The passenger seat had a long tear. The bent steering wheel looked even worse than it had the morning of the accident. And he hadn't remembered the flat front tire or how severely caved in the hood and trunk had been. He checked both bumpers and then examined the rear one again. It was covered in mud that had dried. His mouth felt dry like the mud had found its way into his soul.

He started to wipe the mud away and changed his mind. He pulled out his cell phone, stepped back, and snapped a picture. Then he looked around at Jesse who reached into her purse and handed him a wad of Kleenex. Apparently, she had read his mind.

He started wiping. As the mud began to crumble away, he moved faster, felt his heart racing. The bumper guard on the left and a portion of the lower bumper had a scrape that ran from the center to the left edge. With mud covering it, the scrape had not been visible the night of the accident. But he'd sensed it and made an error in judgment for not pursuing it then. He took another photograph and then bent down and using his Leatherman, scraped the flat tan paint. It flaked off onto the ground fairly easily from the black rubber guards.

"You have anything in your purse so I can collect some of this? I don't need much."

Jesse rummaged through her purse again. She found something suitable. "I knew this would come in handy someday." She ripped the package open, removed the condom and pressed it up to her lips and blew. She held it out.

"Very clever. I think this is going to take the two of us. Just hold it open, underneath where I scrape. Try to catch as much of the paint as you can."

"You're sure it's paint and not mud?"

"It's paint."

Jesse squatted down, teetering on the uneven terrain.

"I think this will prove there was a second vehicle involved."

She tried to positon the condom underneath the bumper. "Let me stretch this thing open some more," she said and gave it a little tug. She then leaned in and held it in place again. "That's better. OK — scrape away."

Between the two of them they managed to fill the tip with tan paint flakes.

Colefield stood holding the goods. With his free hand he bent down and brushed his pant legs. Jesse remained down on her knees.

They both heard the sound of crunching gravel underfoot. Colefield was brushing dirt off the front of his pants when the equipment operator stepped out beside the car. He had a strange look on his face as he stared at the trophy condom.

"That's disgusting..." he stammered and stormed off.

Jesse smiled at Colefield. He helped her to her feet. "It'll give him something to talk about."

Colefield handed Jesse the condom. "Tie a knot in it and then stick it inside your purse."

Jesse deposited the condom and then walked over to the passenger door and looked inside the car.

She pointed to the keyring. "I want the rabbit's foot. It was a present from me to Sis years ago. Maybe it'll help bring her around if she holds it."

"Good thinking." Colefield put down his phone and carefully leaned through the shattered window, and managed to snag the keys without drawing blood.

"Look, I know it's none of my business. The condom sort of got me thinking ... if you don't have your equipment left, why do you have one?"

24

J esse's mood remained sullen. But once they had driven a few miles, her eyes began to brighten, her expression softened, and the look of hurt dissipated. Colefield tried small talk to bring her around, and it was starting to work, so he broadened his horizons.

"I'm sorry, Jesse. I thought you wanted to be with women."

"I want to be a woman, not be with one."

"It's a steep learning curve, I guess."

Jesse looked out the window and sighed. "Where're we going now?"

"Since we're close by, I'd like to make a quick stop at a place called Womack Machine Industries."

Five minutes later the pickup pulled into a wide driveway of a heavy industrial complex that looked like it had been closed for some time. It was comprised of a large concrete building that once was probably the color of the summer sky but now looked washed out, its walls chipped and aged. In front was a shipping dock with two ramps for semi-tractor trailers to load and offload cargo. An office building sat to the left of the main entrance. A chain-link fence surrounded the property with a padlocked gate to keep out intruders. Faded "For Lease" signs were wired to the gate and placed inside the office windows. There was also a realtor's rusted lockbox hanging on the fence.

Colefield took it all in and eventually made a U-turn and headed back out the driveway toward Marine Drive.

"What was that about?"

"The homeless guy I mentioned, his sailboat is registered to this address."

"Are we piecing together some clues, deputy?"

"This was a vital company up until a few years ago. Made millions. Then, according to the articles I read, it suffered a major setback when it lost several of its larger contracts. It went through layoffs, a number of personnel changes but never recovered."

"And this all has to do with what?"

"The son of the owner."

"And he would be?"

"Richard Raulings."

"And who is this Mr. Raulings?"

"He pulled your sister from the wreckage."

"I'm going to give him a big kiss when I meet him."

"According to the articles, his father retired to Hawaii a very wealthy man."

"Then why is his son homeless?"

"I hope to find that out."

Jesse stared out the window, watching a few cars go by.

"If you're up to it," Colefield said. "I'll take you to the accident scene. I want to recheck the area to see if I missed something. When we're through there, I'll need to stop by the office for a few minutes. How long are you staying in town?"

"I'm here for the long haul. I'm not the type to just pop in, check on Sis, and then split. And just so you know, I'll be staying at the houseboat. Before the accident she told me where she keeps a guest key. I understand she hasn't moved in yet, so I imagine the place is pretty empty. I want to get it ready for her to come home to. We're going to be neighbors."

"You're going to need a few things."

"What do you mean?"

"Her place is completely empty, except for a few clothes."

"So, you've already been in it?"

Colefield thought over what he'd said. "No. I was referring to what she told me on the deck that day."

"You're a terrible liar, deputy."

"It was police business."

"You wouldn't last a minute under interrogation."

"You might be surprised."

"Did you have sex, too?"

Colefield coughed.

"That's what I thought."

"What? I didn't say anything?"

"You didn't have to. She's probably too intellectual for you anyway. No, the type of woman you go for has to be outdoorsy, kind of tomboyish, not overly smart, happy-go-lucky, and be willing to pay her own way."

"You left out that she also has to be a Bengals fan."

"Bengals? You really are a loser."

Colefield diverted off football. "I liked Nicole the moment we met. It didn't go anywhere beyond a friendly conversation."

"She's not your type. Trust me."

Colefield concentrated on driving while Jesse stared out the window. A narrow channel ran along the highway with houseboats moored along the northern bank.

"You like working for the River Patrol?"

"I do."

"A person should like what they do for a living. Sis always liked to say: 'If you find work that you love, you'll never work another day in your life.' That's why I'm in between jobs at the moment. For years, I didn't take her advice."

"What kind of work did you do?"

"Chemical Engineering."

"And you didn't like it?"

"It had its moments. I worked for Chevron for six years. But we didn't see eye to eye any longer."

"How 'bout before that?"

"After I gave up trying to be a legal secretary, you mean? That was a long time before I made the change. I discovered very early that attorneys tend to prefer blondes with big tits."

"You could dye your hair."

Jesse ignored the comment. "I barely remember what the attraction of the job had been beyond my interest in civil rights. Somewhere along the way, I took a different path. I have regrets but that is not one of them. I don't have a clue what I'm going to do next. I've got enough cash stashed to last me a while so I can figure it out."

"Everybody deserves a do over," Colefield said, thinking of Jill.

"What about you, Deputy? You enjoy playing cops and robbers?"

"More or less. Being a cop suits me. And I enjoy working and living on the water."

"Deputy, we're more alike than you think."

Colefield changed the subject. "Let's get back to the case. Did you speak with any of her friends after I called you?"

"Two. The day of her accident, they flew out on earlier flights and took cabs. They said Nicole was fine when they left. They didn't seem the least bit concerned about her safety."

"What about Grace?"

"I haven't heard from Grace."

"I spoke with her. She knows. She gave me your cell number."

"Grace is probably taking it pretty hard. She'll call when she can process it. She's in the middle of a divorce and child custody hearings. She's got a pretty full plate."

"There something else I want to ask you. But it can wait..."

The old pickup crossed over I-5 and looped back under the overpass, hooking up with another section of Marine Drive. It rumbled past the golf course and followed the

Multnomah channel. Jesse stared out the front windshield her eye on the expanse of water ahead.

Colefield glanced out the window and did a double-take when he saw a Jet Ski dart by on the channel. But it wasn't who he thought it was. This was a young girl in a wet suit, long hair whipping about in the breeze. It got him thinking though. Then the Sextant appeared and he looked for Jill's Subaru. It was there. He pointed out the River Patrol Headquarters as they drove by. A few miles down the road they pulled onto the shoulder and parked.

Traffic was heavy in both directions. They had to wait for a series of cars to drive by before it was clear to cross.

Jesse stopped and looked down over the embankment toward the river. The current was about 3 to 4 knots, Colefield figured. Little current eddies twirling on the surface of the gray water. A log drifted by with a crow sitting atop it.

"So, this is the spot?"

"This is it," Colefield said.

He checked the pavement. There were traces of gravel and dirt scattered here and there along the shoulder of the road. "When I dove that night searching for her vehicle, it was resting along the river bottom, flipped over on its top. You saw the way it looked at the yard. It's amazing she got out."

"Where did you find her?"

"Over to your right, about a hundred yards or so along the bank. See the patch of tall reeds?"

He pointed out the location and noticed his hand was unsteady. He tried to hide it from Jesse as she walked by him. When they drew up to the spot, he saw her impression still left in the grass and felt nauseous.

Jesse nodded toward it. "Right there?"

Colefield uttered: "Yes."

Jesse bowed her head, closed her eyes and mumbled something that Colefield thought sounded like a prayer. Then she looked out at the river, a few tears running down her face.

"She's always been a good swimmer. In high school, she competed in the 100 meter. And she liked to body surf down in Southern California. But that's been a number of years ago. I want to meet the angel who helped her to shore. Promise me that."

"He's tough to pin down."

"Maybe he's out looking for whoever caused the accident."

"Given his background that could be a strong possibility."

"So, you know more about this Richard Raulings than you're telling me?"

"Yes."

Jesse sighed. "I've seen enough."

They walked along the shoulder and back and whenever there was a break in traffic both looked along Marine Drive for signs of skid marks. Colefield spotted a set about six feet long and stopped. When he did the measurements in his head, the area where the tire marks were didn't match with the line of sight projection the vehicle would have had to make to end up where it did. He didn't see that she tried to brake.

Jesse was up ahead, looking over at a drainage ditch. "There's a dead possum here," she shouted. "Was that here the night of the accident?"

"No."

"Maybe she swerved to miss one and went off the embankment?"

"You're an optimist. I like that about you."

"I wasn't always that way."

"Did she ever mention her clients?"

"Nicole takes her job seriously. She would feel it was a violation of ethics."

"You heard me mention to Dr. Rosin that she asked me if I was for hire as a bodyguard? I found a journal of hers. It contained clinical notes. Several of her clients she was treating at the VA were dangerously unbalanced."

"I can't stop seeing red dots. I'm so scared for her."

"We have several suspects. We just need to narrow it down to the right one."

25

Back at River Patrol Headquarters, Colefield couldn't shake the lurid images of Nicole's accident. Sweating, he wiped his forehead and began introducing Jesse to the rest of the crew when the front door opened, and Detective Feinstein plodded in. Colefield noticed the stocky detective wasn't his normal cheerful self.

"Hey, Colefield, got a minute?"

Colefield nodded and then turned to Bart. "Why don't you give Jesse a tour of the place?"

Bart slid back his chair. "It would be my pleasure."

Jesse took a step forward and stopped. She reached inside her purse and pulled out the condom containing the paint chips. "I'd better give this to you before something happens to it."

Everyone in the office stared.

"Bart," Colefield said. "Take that and run it downtown for analysis. Fill out a Chain-of-Custody. Leave the first couple lines blank. I'll fill them in before you leave."

Bart grimaced. "This will be a first."

He walked over and reluctantly plucked the condom from Jesse's hand while Colefield followed Feinstein outside.

In the parking lot, the detective dug out a pack of smokes from his shirt pocket. "That's an interesting piece of evidence."

He took his time pulling out a cigarette before placing it between his lips. He didn't light it. "I heard you were prying into the administrator's case..."

"Word gets around fast."

"I saw footage of you in the parking lot asking a lot of questions."

"The administrator had the room across from Nicole Dafoe."

"And you think there's a connection to the Dafoe incident?"

The detective put the cigarette back in the pack and stuffed it inside his pocket. "VA wants to sweep this under the rug. They're worried about PR."

Colefield paused. "You still in good with Judge Abraham?"

"You want me to subpoena records?"

"Nicole Dafoe was attacked. They may not be done with her. And I suspect we've seen this killer's work before."

"Some gray area here."

"No one is arguing that."

"The brother give you anything?"

"SHE didn't know her sister was in any danger."

"They get along?"

"Says they do."

"Is her sister conscious yet?"

"No."

"I'll see what I can do. In the meantime, keep me in the loop."

Feinstein started to leave. Colefield called out: "Hey, I may have something."

The detective turned. Colefield walked over to him. "I've had several encounters with a guy by the name of Richard Raulings. He's a homeless guy, lives on the river. He claims he rescued Nicole and knows who tried to kill her."

"And I'm just hearing about this now? How long have you been sitting on this?"

"He showed me an old article about Christian Riker and claims he's the guy responsible."

"Have you talked with Riker?"

"Working on that."

"Your evidence inside have something to do with him?"

"It may confirm he owns a tan Hummer that was involved in the accident."

After the detective left, Colefield went back inside. Jesse and Bart were in the garage. Colefield could hear their voices. Weaver was working on a report at his desk. He stopped what he was doing and sat back in his chair.

"I think Bart is smitten."

Colefield stopped at the window and looked out. "Where's Tony?"

"Willamette office."

"I've got to run Jesse back to the hospital. After Bart drops off the sample at the lab, you guys take the sled and see if you can locate Raulings. But be careful and call in backup if necessary."

Across the room the rear door from the garage swung open. Jesse popped into the office smiling followed by Bart. They moved toward the center of the room.

"Bart showed me all the equipment you boys use on your rescue operations. Mighty impressive."

"Jesse wants to go on patrol."

"It sounds fun."

Colefield shook his head. "Another time, Jesse. We need to keep focused on the job. And you are too much of a pleasant distraction."

26

Out in the parking lot, Colefield slammed the driver's door and dug around in his pocket for the ignition key.

"Something the matter?"

He shook his head and stuck the bent key into the old Ford's ignition switch. "Feel like a drink?"

"Thought you'd never ask."

Colefield remembered he hadn't filled in his section of the Chain-of-Custody Form.

"I'll be right back."

Jesse reached into her purse and pulled out her compact, checked her makeup. Then she pulled out her cellphone, checked for messages, and leaned out the open passenger window just as the deputy was reaching the front door. "What about that place over there?" She pointed to the Sextant Restaurant.

It was convenient, but Jill was working.

"They have lousy service," he said.

"How's the beer?"

"Not much better."

"OK. What's the real reason you don't want to go there? I saw you checking out the parking lot earlier."

The restaurant was packed. A hectic staff dashed around with trays of beer and greasy food, trying to keep hunger at bay. The aroma smelled of French fries and sizzling meat. Colefield could almost see the deep-fat fryers boiling in the kitchen. And it's what made the place great — handcut fries and a fat juicy hamburger to sink your teeth in.

Jesse marched right up to the bar and gave the place a once over. Colefield followed a few paces behind. He spotted Jill behind the bar but she didn't look over and catch his eye. It was just as well.

"There's a seat by the window. Go lock it down for us, honey," Jesse said. "I'm going to the little girl's room."

Colefield crossed the room and sat down at the small table. The bar was in plain view. Jill was slinging drinks at the waitress station lined three-deep with hustling staff.

He glanced over at the bar out of habit and this time caught Jill's eye. She stared back between drinks and almost smiled. About then, Jesse walked up to the table and planted herself across from him.

Jill's smile turned into a scowl.

"It's the bartender, isn't it?" Jesse asked.

"It is."

"I figured that out the moment I walked in. She's definitely got the Tomboy look going. You need some dating tips though."

"Really?"

"Why didn't you say hello when we came in?"

"She's busy."

"No woman is that busy, honey."

"Quit with the honey business. It's deputy or Jason."

Jesse frowned. "What's her name?"

"Jill."

"Well, Jill is a spritely angel. I can see why you would be attracted to her."

"Thank you."

"Now go say hello before she gets the wrong impression about us."

Colefield grimaced, stood up, and approached the bar, dodging a waitress juggling a full tray of drinks. Jill saw him immediately. She wiped her hands on her apron and tipped back her cowboy hat, a trickle of perspiration on her brow.

"Really, Jason! As if I don't have enough on my mind and then you bring your latest floosy in to rub in my face."

"She's —"

But before he could finish his sentence, a different waitress slid in front of him with an empty tray of glassware, nudging him aside, and dropping the heavy tray down on the bar.

"Hey, Jason."

"Hello, Becky."

"Jill says you two are on the rocks; that true?"

Colefield looked back at Jill. "She's not my date, Jill. I came over to say 'hello'."

"Becky, honey, what do you need?" Jill asked.

"Three Fat Tires, a Heineken, two rum-and-cokes. One with lime."

Another waitress squeezed up to the waitress station and nudged in. "Hey, Jason. Where's Bart?"

"Work."

"Tell him I said 'hello'."

He looked over at Jill juggling glasses under the taps. "Can we talk sometime?"

She kept her back to him. "In this lifetime?"

Colefield gave up and walked off. When he sat back down, Jesse smiled reluctantly. "Didn't go so well, did it?"

"At least she didn't pull a knife."

"She's done that?"

"Don't ask."

"Well, she just needs a man to take charge."

"You're reading her wrong."

"Never," she said. "Trust me on this. That girl loves you."

"She has a strange way of showing it."

"Maybe it's you who has the problem showing it."

"What do you want to drink?"

"I thought I'd order some food too – greasiest cheese burger this joint makes. I'm starving. What do you recommend on tap?"

"Fat Tire."

"What are you having?"

"A coke. I'm still on duty."

Jesse was almost done with her meal when Jill walked up to the table. She still had on her apron but she wasn't frowning. Things had slowed behind the bar and she was helping bus tables. She stopped and picked up her empty plate. She smiled down at Jesse. "I don't think I've seen you in here before. My name's Jill. What's your name, honey?"

"Jesse Dafoe."

"Dafoe, that name rings a bell."

Jason kept his eye on her and his mouth shut. He would have said a prayer if he thought it would do any good.

"Oh, my God!" Jill uttered, glaring at him. "You Son-of-a-bitch!" And with that, she stormed off with a lethal-load of dirty plates.

"Well, looks like you're batting 100 today," Jesse said. "What was that about?"

"Your sister stopped in here the night of her accident."

"Why didn't you mention this earlier?"

"I was going to get around to it."

"No wonder that poor darling shriveled up like she'd been gut-punched. She served Nicole, didn't she? And you came in here afterward and told her?"

"Yep."

"Deputy, what am I going to do with you? She must just feel —"

Jesse's cell phone rang and cut her off mid-sentence. Before she could answer it, Colefield's cell phone rang. They both answered them simultaneously.

Neither seemed able to make out what the other was talking about. Then Jesse let out a scream and jumped up and gave Jason a big hug. Nicole was conscious, her fog had lifted.

Somewhere over near the kitchen, a load of plates smashed on the floor.

27

J esse was a nervous wreck before they arrived at the
hospital. "What if she isn't the same? What if she can't
remember me? What if she's *malato*?"

"What?"

"An invalid. Mental. Drooling out of the side of her
mouth."

Colefield recognized the doctor standing over Nicole's
hospital bed when he followed Jesse into the room and closed
the door.

"Dr. Phillip, how's she doing?" Colefield asked.

The young doctor closed her chart and put her pen in her
pocket. She turned and gave them both a friendly smile. "See
for yourself."

She stepped back from the bed and Nicole Dafoe's face
brightened. "Hey, Sis — what a nice surprise." Her voice was
weak. "When did you get in town?" She turned and looked at
Colefield. "Who's your friend?"

Dr. Phillip moved aside allowing Jesse to slip by and give
her sister a hug. She nodded to Colefield to join her in the
hallway.

After the door closed, Dr. Phillip turned to Colefield. Her
expression was firm and professional: "She hasn't regained all
her memory. It's her body's way of expressing trauma. She
knows her identity. Her memory, facts, emotions and personal
biography seem intact. They're stored in different parts of the
brain and retrieved via different pathways. Her memory loss

appears to be temporal to the day of the accident. I'll let you have ten minutes with her."

"So, she doesn't remember anything about the accident?"

"No. Don't expect much. It could be weeks or months before we see progress."

"Thanks, doctor."

"Ten minutes."

"Who else knows that she has regained consciousness?"

"Just the nursing staff."

"If it goes public, there's the possibility the person trying to do her harm may attempt to finish the job."

"I'll alert security."

"How long before she can leave here?"

"I'd like to hold her for a few more days."

"Do what you have to. But keep reporters out of her corridor."

"I'll tell the staff to be vigilant."

The doctor checked her watch. "Ten minutes, deputy. The clock starts now."

Colefield entered the room. He stopped at the end of the bed and waited. Jesse had moved a chair beside the bed and was holding Nicole's hand, talking in a soft voice.

Nicole sat up. "Who's this handsome, devil?" she asked.

"Hello, Nicole. I'm Deputy Jason Colefield. We met the other day down at the marina. I'm your neighbor. Do you remember me?"

Nicole's eyes studied him. "No, I'm afraid I don't. Did we meet at a marina in San Francisco?"

"No, Ma'am. At the Portland Rowing Club. I live in tender 12A."

"I'm confused..."

Jesse turned and raised her eyebrows.

Nicole's tone became serious. "Would someone mind telling me how I got here?"

"You had an accident." Colefield moved closer to the bed.

Jesse reached out and pushed a strand of hair from Nicole's face revealing fresh stitches. "You drove off the road, honey, and ended up in the river. That's how you got that nasty bump on your head."

Nicole's face went blank.

"The deputy and I visited the impound yard where they took your car. It's a complete total, Sis. It's a miracle you got out alive."

"I wrecked my car?"

"I'm afraid so," Colefield said, suddenly sad. "I was the diver for the River Patrol who went down to recover it."

"What happened?"

Colefield checked his watch. "We were hoping you could tell us."

"The last thing I remember was being at work."

"Did any of your patients threaten you recently?" Colefield asked.

Nicole closed her eyes and appeared to be thinking about the question. Her eyes reopened with more darkness behind them. "There was this young man who made me extremely uncomfortable during one of our sessions. It's nothing that he did, you understand, but in my line of work, what one doesn't do can be just as revealing..."

"What's his name, honey?" Jesse asked.

The door across the room opened and Dr. Phillip stopped just inside the door and tapped her wristwatch.

"Honey, your doctor needs us to leave now. But we'll be back soon. Try and get some rest."

Colefield knew he had gone past his allotted time but he still had questions. "Do the initials JR, YB, BN or ZE mean anything to you?"

"Where's my purse?" Nicole asked.

Dr. Phillip sighed and pointed to the closet. Without acknowledging her obvious disapproval, Colefield opened the door and removed the same black purse he had searched through the night of the accident. The leather still felt wet. Colefield handed Jesse the purse. She placed it on her lap and then looked over at her sister. "What am I looking for?" she asked Nicole.

Nicole sat up straighter. "My wallet. I want to give you my hotel room key."

Jesse reached in and removed a black wallet. She held it out. Nicole started to reach for it and pulled back suddenly. "I'm sorry, I'm feeling nauseous. Jesse, could you please look for it." Jesse looked at Dr. Phillip.

"Nicole — besides the nausea," Dr. Phillip said, "do you have other pains?"

"My head is screaming. And there is something wrong with my ribs."

"We didn't see any fractures on your chest x-rays. You do have some severe bruising of your upper abdominal cavity. I'll see what I can do to relieve your discomfort."

Jesse frowned at Colefield then dug through her sister's wallet until she found a hotel key, took it out and handed it to him. Jesse set the purse on her lap while Nicole laid her head back against the pillow and closed her eyes.

"What hotel, dear?"

Nicole opened her eyes and gazed up at her sister with a pained expression. "The Mark Spencer."

28

The historic Mark Spenser Hotel sat on the corner of SW 11th and Stark. It was a six-story brick building with a certain European charm, which included a wrought iron gated entrance. Plenty of foliage made an inviting walkway up to the front door. And the convenience of Kenny and Zukes Restaurant, a New York styled deli across the street, seemed like a good fit for a busy psychiatrist. The hotel catered to long term tenancies.

Jesse walked through the large glass doors and headed in the general direction of the front desk. Colefield let her handle the clerk while he walked around and checked things out.

He spotted a small library within view of the front desk, strolled in and glanced at a few paperbacks on one of the shelves, thumbed through a stack of magazines, looked at where the exits were, and then moved into the hallway.

Jesse was patiently waiting while the attendant finished up on the telephone. She glanced back and saw Colefield keeping an eye on her and winked. About that time the clerk placed the receiver on its cradle and looked up.

"Yes, how can I help you?" he asked.

"I believe you have a Nicole Dafoe that is staying here."

"We haven't seen Ms. Dafoe for several days. Is she all right?"

"She's had an automobile accident." Jesse pulled out her wallet and showed the man her driver's license. "I'm her sister."

"How awful!"

Colefield stepped up. "Does she have any messages?"

The clerk spun around and checked the box with her room number. She had four or five pieces of mail which he handed to Jesse.

"I'll need to rekey the card. Could I see it?"

Jesse handed it to him and waited.

They got off on the top floor. Colefield glanced up at the brass room numbers on the wall and let Jesse lead the way. The hallways were narrow, newly painted with the scent of turpentine lingering, and colorful new carpet. When they reached the door, Jesse stuck the keycard into the door lock, waited for the beep to sound and the green light to blink on. As soon as it did, Colefield moved her aside, motioned for her to wait in the hall, and gave the door a firm push and went inside. Once the door was closed, Colefield looked around for a light switch, found it and flipped it on. He was relieved to see the room didn't have any unexpected guests.

He opened the door and told Jesse to come inside.

The room lit up into a yellowish glow. The small entryway, immediately opened into a kitchenette equipped with a refrigerator and stove, along with cutlery. A door on the left led to the bedroom with a full bath attached. The room was clean, comfortable, charming in a European way. The living room had antique furniture. The blinds were drawn on the windows to keep out the heat. Jesse opened them and let in the bright light. Colefield looked over her shoulder, didn't see any fire escape stairs, and noted the room overlooked Stark Street with a view of the Brewery Blocks in the distance. He could hear light traffic along Burnside.

"Place looks comfy. I googled it on the drive over," Jesse said. "I can see why she stayed here. Lots of artsy and musical types. It's modestly priced with a sense of old charm, without all the lemon oil and fuss, and snooty bellboys with their hands out. Sis can be a very practical girl when it comes to her wallet…"

"She never mentioned this place?"

"Not a peep."

"You think she was keeping it from you?"

"I don't feel it was so much that. She talked mostly of the city and how much fun she was having exploring downtown and the Pearl District. She rarely mentioned work. When I called her the day of her party, she touched on the new house she had purchased and you of course. I guess I'm to blame. Most of the time, I'm pretty self-absorbed."

Colefield walked through the place looking at her personal belongings. She had several books and journals lying on one of the night stands. *War* by Sebastian Junger and *The Heart of Counseling: A guide to Developing Therapeutic Relationships* by Jeff Cochran, two *Journals of Behavioral Medicine*, and *American Sniper* by Chris Kyle. Colefield picked up *War* and thumbed through it looking to see if she had made or left any notes behind. He did the same with the other books and journals.

She had made several notes which were tucked inside one of the journals and *War*. Colefield read them: "Treating combat veterans is different from treating rape victims, because rape victims don't have this idea that some aspects of their experience are worth retaining."

And another: "PTSD is a crisis of connection and disruption, not an illness you carry inside you."

The last one struck a deeper chord. "Though only 10 percent of American forces see combat, the U.S. military now has the highest rate of post-traumatic stress disorder in its history."

He knew, because he was one of them...

He put the notes back where he found them and moved on.

One drawer in her bedroom had some stationary and writing tablets in it. He thumbed through the pages of the tablet but they were empty.

Another drawer held a few sweaters and a San Francisco 49's sweatshirt.

The third drawer held some gym shorts and T-shirts.

He found a briefcase under the bed. He pulled it out and set it down on the bedspread. It was brown leather with spinning brass locks on each side. Jesse walked into the room with an empty paper bag that she had found in one of the kitchen cabinets.

"Is it unlocked?"

"I'm about to find out."

Colefield squeezed the latches. The locks sprung open. The briefcase held closing documents from the purchase of the houseboat down at his marina. There were also credit card receipts, rent receipts, and some credit card bills all paid in full. There was nothing related to work or case files, which is what he was hoping to find.

He closed the briefcase and returned it to where he found it.

"She's a very neat person," Jesse said. "I used to get whipped as a kid because my room was so messy. Nicole was always the type of person who made her bed first thing when she woke up. She never left anything lying around. She was not rebellious by nature like I was. She did what she was told and excelled at everything. I was just the opposite. I'm better as a woman now. I'm not this organized or tidy by any means but I'm nothing like I was as a boy."

"I'll let you get her things together out of the bathroom. I'm about done here, unless I find something out of place."

Colefield snooped through the cupboards and glanced inside the refrigerator. The freezer held two bags of frozen green beans and a package of frozen halibut. On the shelves were organic brown eggs, humus, yogurt, pita bread, almond butter, and more healthy stuff. She took vitamins, appeared to eat well, and didn't appear to have a drug or alcohol problem. What the hell was he missing? Nobody was this perfect. Then he found a drawer full of Girl Scout cookies. Ah, a weakness…

Jesse walked out carrying the paper bag. She handed it to Colefield and then returned to the bedroom for some more items. Colefield glanced inside. It held a couple pair of panties, a tank top, and some socks, shampoo and other hygiene items. Jesse reappeared carrying a hanger with a blue short-sleeve blouse and a pair of black slip-on pants.

"I think I got everything," she said. "You ready?"

Colefield popped one of the cookies into his mouth and nodded.

29

After he finished his shift at work, he headed toward home. It was getting dark. He was beat and just wanted to kick back, have a beer or two.

He became aware of being followed as he made his way down the metal ramp leading to the houseboats. He put his hand on his holster and spun around.

The person was wearing a baby blue ski jacket, tight jeans, and cowboy boots. She had a bottle of beer in her right hand; in her left she carried what was left of a six-pack.

"Care for a beer, deputy?"

She strolled toward him. Her breath smelled of alcohol and peppermints but she didn't appear drunk. "Here!" she said, handing him the six-pack. "It's not your favorite but it's cold."

Colefield didn't know what to say. It'd been months since Jill had been to the tender. It wasn't all that tidy. But she'd have to just turn a blind eye. This unexpected visit had him a little on edge. He couldn't believe he hadn't spotted her in the lot.

He pushed open the front door. The place was dark. He hadn't left on a night light and wondered if Calico Jack was inside waiting to be fed.

"Watch your step. There might be a cat down by your feet."

"You have a cat?"

Colefield flipped on the light switch. The room lit up with a hazy glow. He set the six-pack down on the kitchen counter, took out one of the bottles and opened it with his key chain.

"You need another?" he asked.

Jill threw back her head and guzzled hers down. She dropped the empty down on the counter, peeled off her jacket and tossed it on a wooden chair by the door. "I can't remember where the bathroom is."

"It's the first door to your right."

"I'll take another beer."

Jill wandered off toward the bathroom. After a few minutes Colefield heard the toilet flush. He looked around the floor but didn't see Calico Jack anywhere. He opened a can of cat food, dumped it into a bowl, placed it on the floor and filled the cat's water dish. After that he walked into the living room and turned on a brass pole lamp and put on some soft music. Jill was taking her sweet time in the head.

Then he heard the shower come on. He walked over to the door and looked in. He watched Jill pull her tank top over her head and unstrap her bra, which she let fall to the floor around her bare feet.

"The towels are in the cabinet below the sink," he said through the door.

"Where's your shampoo?"

"It's in the stall."

"Are you coming in or are you going to gawk at me through the crack in the door?"

He didn't know what he wanted to do, to be honest. Finally, he turned the door knob and went inside.

Steam rushed at his eyes. He remembered Jill liked a very hot shower. That was her thing. She stood under the steam soaping her hair. Colefield leaned back on the bathroom counter and admired her small perky breasts and defined curves. Her narrow waist and long legs still didn't have a mark

on them. No tattoos, no scars. Just smooth tanned hide that
reminded him how lucky he was to be standing there.

She rinsed the soap from her hair and looked at him.

"I'll turn it down for you," she said.

Colefield set his beer down and began to undress. It'd
been so long, he wondered if he could quell his restless spirit
and enjoy her sensual touch. If he could lose himself, find the
courage to really let go this time, pry back the doors of a heart
that seemed rusted shut, then maybe he wouldn't end up a
fallen soldier or another River Rat, isolated, detached from
human contact, at war with himself. Once he was naked, she
pulled the curtain back inviting him in. He stepped in behind
her, breathed in her womanly scent and savored it. She
dropped a bar of soap into his hand and turned her back
toward him.

He moved in closer, ran the soap from her slender neck,
down the deep ridge of her spine to the contours of her
buttocks. He rubbed the bar between his hands to soap them
up and then glided them down sliding them along the inside of
her firm thighs. She opened her legs wider. He massaged the
hollow spot behind her knees. Then he squatted and soaped
each one of her feet before he spun her around and worked
the soap back up her front side, stopping at her pubic area. He
began to soap her small dark bush. Her eyes indicated she
liked what he was doing. He slid the tip of his middle finger
inside the warm flesh, and then went deeper. He felt her stir.
He eased the finger out and ran the bar of soap up her
stomach, along the underside of her breasts, and up over her
nipples. She let out a little cry and he let the water cascade
down on her, washing off the suds. He then leaned down and
kissed the underside of her neck and moved his lips along her
warm skin to her mouth. She bit down on his lower lip, just to
the point of breaking the skin before she released. She took
the bar of soap from him, pushed him against the stall wall and
ran the bar over his penis. He felt himself harden. He sensed

her power over him and so did she. She pressed her breasts against his chest and kissed him hard on the lips. She ran her hand down over his scars and then stopped. Her eyes filled with a hurtful hunger.

She stepped out of the shower. And quickly removed a towel from beneath the counter and patted her face, arms, and chest dry all the while her dark eyes sized him up in the mirror. Then she gathered up her clothing, reached over, took the beer off the counter and left.

When he came out of the bathroom a minute later, she was not in the living room or the kitchen. He spotted her jacket on the chair where she'd left it and felt relieved. There was only one place left to look.

He headed down the hall toward the bedroom.

30

Colefield woke late the following morning to an empty bed. He listened for sounds of her moving about the tender but didn't hear anything other than fireworks exploding on someone's deck. He didn't know whether to be relieved or hurt. He was leaning toward a love hangover. Again.

He glanced at the night stand but she hadn't left behind a note. But then what did he expect her to say? They weren't really the sweet love note type. He checked the clock. Hell, he'd overslept. He jumped out of bed, threw on some clean clothes, and headed for the bathroom.

Outside, it was the 4th of July crowd. Residents of the marina were having a gay old time with their fireworks. He heard what sounded like an M80, a quarter stick of dynamite, thunder down off Montgomery's deck and figured his landlord was up to his old tricks.

There was a damp towel lying on the bathroom floor. He picked it up and smelled its lingering soapy scent. It all came rushing back. The memory of her warm flesh pressed against his. The way their bodies fit so nicely together in bed. Last night during some tender moments, he caught her eyes drilling into him.

"What's up, Jill?"

"I've been worried about you Jason, worried about us." There was urgency to her voice. "I feel at times I don't know who you are anymore. You take two steps forward and then when I try to move with you, you take two steps back."

Her words hit a painful cord. "I've never talked to you about my PTSD. It was always something I felt I had a handle on — something I could control. After my time in the Navy, it lay below the surface but didn't get in the way. But lately, I don't know any longer. These feelings of anger, frustration, alienation, are squeezing down on me. I know what triggered it. It's all the veterans involved in this case and a survivalist soldier who I've come to admire and fear. I could become him. And I don't want to. I could be like Montgomery. And I don't want to be him either. Do you understand any of this?"

Her eyes softened. "I'm beginning to."

"I've been seeing a VA counselor."

"Seeing — meaning you on a sofa and they're behind a desk?"

"Of course. I'll get through this rough patch. I promise you that." It felt like something broke in him, releasing a pocket of darkness.

"We'll find answers together. I love you, Deputy Colefield."

There was a glimmer of light ahead. He leaned in and kissed her and felt tears both his and hers mingling like moonlight on a misty landscape.

He turned on the faucet and threw some cold water on his face and then looked at his unshaven reflection in the mirror. Something about him looked different, younger perhaps, less stress lines under his eyes.

Then his mind flipped back to when she was standing there. Her lovely body simmering in the hot shower; her nakedness, so inviting, highlighted by the glistening water droplets, diamond crystals sprinkling her chest, back and thighs.

The memory and towel were not all she had left behind. A single fresh lipstick kiss was imprinted on the mirror, which brought a smile to his face. Maybe just maybe they had a second chance.

Out in the kitchen he spotted some fresh cat hairs where she had left her jacket on the chair the night before and he found an empty almond milk container on the counter. He pulled open the refrigerator. The partial six-pack was inside next to an open can of cat food.

What a night...

Changing gears Colefield headed to interview Nicole Dafoe. Jesse had left a message that she was doing better, and had begun eating some liquids. The doctors seemed to think she might be able to leave the hospital soon.

Jesse was waiting outside her door.

"Does she remember any more about the accident?" Colefield asked.

"No."

"Maybe she never will."

"Perhaps if she sees you again, it'll jog her memory." Jesse cocked her head. "You look different today. Like you might have ... did you have company last night?"

Colefield's jaw dropped.

"It was that cute tomboy from the Sextant, wasn't it?"

"I guess she wasn't all that pissed off."

"Oh, yes she was. We girls just have an interesting way of expressing it sometimes."

31

A few hours later in the heat of the late afternoon sun, Bart had the wheel of the patrol boat headed toward McGuire Island. Weaver was struggling to read his iPhone screen, which was jiggling around in his hand. Colefield sat on the starboard side of the boat, thinking about the information he had obtained from Dr. Rosin.

"Find anything, Weaver?"

"If Bart would slow down, I could read the screen better. But I think I got something here."

Weaver read it off. "Raulings is from the Northwest. He graduated from Lincoln High School and went to Georgia Tech on a football scholarship. Played ball for two years then joined the Marines in 2004. He served 8 years and was honorably discharged in 2012. Numerous deployments in Iraq, Afghanistan and Bangladesh. There's more. He was outstanding as a quarterback. Georgia Tech had their best years while he played for them."

"Mention anything about why he left school?"

"Give me a minute." He continued reading. "Apparently, he had an uncle serving in the military who encouraged him to join."

Bart cut in. "They'll be a handful of reservists that'll help patrol the island after the fireworks at Fort Vancouver tonight. Washington has their river patrol out too. We can call in plenty of backup if we need to."

Colefield rubbed his eyes. "Our job is to find this guy before things heat up with the parties on Government Island.

Harv is going to let us know if he finds either one of the other vets from Dr. Dafoe's group. He's got patrolmen canvasing the streets and he's heading out to the address of record for JR and his brother. They live in a cabin along the Sandy River. I wrote the address down. It's in my pocket. Once we bring in Raulings, we can offer Harv a hand if the brothers don't cooperate."

Even from the center of the river, Colefield could see the large crowds of campers and day-boaters dotting the shoreline. An array of colorful tents sprinkled the hillside all the way down to the beach. A stage was set up along the southern side of the island in the heart of the crowd. Rock music thundered from six enormous speakers set up along the sides of the stage. Fireworks crackled here and there, sparklers fizzled out down by the water. Bikini clad women danced around in the sun as they roared by.

McGuire Island came upon them before they knew it. With the engine down to a purr, the sled idled into the narrow channel and crept back toward the deserted cove. Just like the last time, there were no other boats around. Just the one big flotilla he hoped would still be there.

But Raulings was nowhere to be found.

"Let's go fine Harvey."

32

U priver, the River Patrol boat glided over the short white caps as they entered the narrows. Silver licks of water lashed out at the aluminum hull like schools of summer smelt. To the south the sheer cliffs of Tegart Bluff came into view and then the opening of Chinook Landing.

Bart held onto the helm and guided the boat toward the middle of the river following the deeper waters of the shipping lane. Ahead was the entrance to the Sandy River. Tall reeds and patches of trees along the southern riverbank masked its narrow stem. As a point of reference Colefield used Lady Island to his port in combination with the old smoke stacks of the Camas Paper Mill as the final marker of where to change course.

Today was no different.

Off in the distance the plume of white steam from the massive pulp mill rose above the trees. The young deputy eased back on the throttle. Colefield kept his eye on the depth finder. The numbers were low but Colefield wagered they'd be able to make it.

Here and there logs and limbs appeared but Bart steered clear of them. Colefield pulled out his cell phone and tried Feinstein's number again. There was no signal.

"How much fuel do we have?"

"I topped off the tanks before we left."

The Sandy snaked its way through dense foliage. Craggy oaks lined the banks of the river. As the boat crept closer to Troutdale City Limits an array of festive lights along Main

Street lit up the hint of darkness creeping down upon the landscape. The old water tower painted in graffiti near town center brought back a few memories for Colefield but he pushed them aside and remained focused.

"Bart, call dispatch on the marine radio. Have them patch you through to Homicide. See if Feinstein has made contact within anyone in his office today."

"Roger that."

"Weaver, how are you coming on tracking down Riker's info?"

"His Oregon License is current. No warrants, no tickets. A 2014 tan Hummer is registered to him with no lien-holders. Wait a second and I'll read off the address … maybe we'll get lucky."

When Bart put the mic back in its cradle, he looked over at Colefield, shaking his head. "Feinstein's shift ended hours ago. No one has heard from him. But he's still got a cruiser checked out."

"Riker's vehicle is registered to a business on SE 9th in Milwaukie. Riker Demolition Inc."

Colefield pulled a piece of paper from his pocket and read some scribbles. "See if this address matches what Harv passed on to me this morning. Then look up the older brother, James Riker."

"James' license has a military POB in Afghanistan for Christ's sake."

"Try the parents or any other Riker that may have a Sandy, Oregon address."

After a few minutes, Weaver shouted. "Got it! He's listed under James Christian Riker, 28292A, Historic Columbia River Highway. Looks like Harvey's information is correct."

"Shouldn't be much further," Bart said, and then watched the shallow water approaching beyond Lewis and Clark State Park. Before Bart could alter course, they hit a series of rapids and shallows. Bart held to the main stem off to the left and the boat rocked along under the dull roar of freeway traffic above on I-84.

"We have a problem," Bart yelled.

Colefield stared at the rocks sticking up out of the water ahead just as Bart hit the dead-man switch, cutting the engine while the aluminum hull scraped over the gravel bedrock as it went aground.

33

Colefield couldn't believe their luck. What were the odds? He noticed his hand was trembling when he stepped out of the boat into the shallow water. Weaver gave him a concerned look and then leaned over the gunnel and opened a tackle compartment. He pulled out a coil of braided rope along with a sling, snatch hook, and carabiner. He handed the items to Bart and then reached back inside the compartment and removed a portable gasoline-powered winch.

"Go find a spot to tie off," Colefield ordered Bart.

Colefield focused on what had to be done next. He thought if they could winch the boat forward about thirty feet, they'd be out of the worst of it, since it was too heavy to just pick up and carry over the shallows.

He checked his watch. Daylight wouldn't last much longer. He was starting to fear the worst. Had they been too slow getting the information about Riker? And Raulings hadn't been at his flotilla probably for a damn good reason.

For Christ's sake where the hell was Harvey?

After Bart splashed ashore, he approached a stout cedar trunk and slipped the sling around it. Weaver lugged the winch over and attached to it. Bart walked back toward the boat, playing out a trail of rope behind him.

Colefield had looped a double braided line around the bow cleats. "Fire it up!" he shouted to Weaver.

Weaver started the winch as Colefield and Bart pushed on the stern.

He felt the boat beginning to break loose and pushed harder. "Hold up a minute, Weaver!"

Following the same route upriver and approaching very fast was somebody on a Jet Ski. Colefield turned and gave a warning wave. The jet skier swerved to the opposite side of the river and raced right over the shallows, not losing a beat.

Colefield caught a good glimpse of the man's face. "Son-of-a-bitch! It's Raulings!" Colefield shouted. "Where the hell's he going?"

And then it occurred to him in a flash...

"Raulings is headed to Riker's just like he told us he would."

It seemed to take forever. Eventually, the deputies had the boat moving into deeper water. They threw the tackle aboard, hopped in, and the motor fired on the first try.

"The GPS picking up the address?" Colefield checked the river ahead for any signs of the Jet Ski.

Bart nodded. "We got a couple miles. It's on our port side right after we pass by Shirley's Tippy Canoe Restaurant."

"He's there by now."

The sled began to accelerate and the breeze off the water seemed cooler now after their workout. The river made a bend as they entered another narrow section with swift current. Ahead, the lights of the restaurant acted as a chart marker on the lonely river. The men kept to themselves, each lost in their own thoughts. *Not long now...*

He thought highly of Harvey Feinstein. There were a number of reasons to explain why his friend hadn't called. None of them made him feel any better. His gut told him Harvey was up to his ass in some nasty business.

Structures sprang up on both sides of the riverbank, surrounded by old growth. He pulled out a pair of binoculars and studied the houses perched along the river bank. He didn't see anyone outside. A few interior lights were on but most weren't.

Bart pointed ahead. A large wood cabin came into view, tucked well-back from the shoreline. It sat on a ridge partially hidden inside a pocket of trees. The closest neighbor was beyond shouting distance. And there was a familiar Jet Ski parked near a path that led up to the cabin.

Bart eased off the throttle and nosed the boat toward shore. Just then — a thunderous echo cracked a hole in the heavy silence, startling a flock of blackbirds out of the woods. The birds swooped down across their path, while the deputies fell back into their seats, instinctively reaching for their weapons.

"Holy Shit! What the hell was that?"

Splintered wood and bits of earth rained down on the men and splashed into the river.

Bart managed to beach the boat. Weaver and Colefield shook off the debris, jumped out and scanned the landscape, weapons drawn, while a second cloud of fallout sprinkled down on them from a canopy of trees. On the bluff above, Colefield heard shouts.

The deputies made their way along a dirt path that led up the steep embankment toward the cabin.

At the top, they stopped, crouching down to catch their breath and get the lay of the land.

The property was still smoldering. Colefield could hear excited voices and saw a group of concerned neighbors running down the road in their direction. Bart and Weaver moved toward the smoking ruin.

Feinstein's cruiser was parked by the highway but where was he?

"Over here!" came a shout from the one of the neighbors.

Feinstein was propped up against a tree. At first Colefield thought he was blown to shreds, there was so much blood. As he knelt by his friend, he realized Harvey's body wasn't the source of the carnage. Bloody bits and pieces of human remains had rained down on him.

"Harvey, can you hear me? It's Jason."

The detective's eyes shot open. Feinstein craned his head up and stared at Colefield. Colefield felt his gut knot up. He reached out and plucked a hunk of meat from the detective's head and tossed it aside.

"Hold still," he said.

Colefield conducted a quick examination of his friend. Aside from being covered in bloody debris, he appeared intact.

Bart jogged over excitedly and stopped suddenly a few feet away. He looked over at the detective and then down at the ground. Hunks of skin and bone littered the earth. His eyes widened.

Colefield looked behind him toward the road. A crowd was starting to gather. When he turned around, Weaver stepped out of the woods and stopped a few feet away. "Did you see any other survivors?"

"Negative," Weaver replied.

"Call it in. Keep the neighbors off the property. Stay back at least fifty feet until I say otherwise. This place could be wired."

"Got no arguments from me," Weaver said and walked off cautiously, looking where he stepped.

Feinstein grimaced. "I tried talking the kid out of it."

"Which kid?"

"James."

"James is dead?"

Feinstein nodded.

"What about Christian?"

"He may be dead too."

"Anyone else?"

"Some guy came up from the river. I didn't get a good look at him." The detective coughed. "Maybe he's dead, too."

Fine ash fell around them. The stench of burnt flesh was overwhelming.

Just then a two-stroke engine fired up down along the riverbank. They couldn't see if it was a watercraft or not, but Colefield had his hunches.

"You up to walking?" Colefield asked. "I think we should get out of here."

Feinstein grabbed Colefield's arm. "The sooner the better."

34

It was the middle of the night when he pulled into the Emanuel Hospital parking lot in Feinstein's cruiser. When he glanced down at his hands, they were trembling on the steering wheel.

The bomb squad said the entire property had been rigged with explosives. It was a miracle any of them made it out alive. Someone had cut a few key wires which probably saved the neighborhood from going up in smoke. Colefield figured that had been Rauling's handiwork. They still hadn't accounted for Christian Riker.

Feinstein had been the one to insist he take the cruiser. The cavalry had been called in. The sirens had come and gone. So had the fire department, the police, the ambulance with Feinstein in it, and the State Medical Examiner's Office. Lab techs would be busy processing the remains well into the night. It was still too early to tell if there was more than one body scattered around the property.

His body felt broken, so did his spirit. Everything looked askew, the lights of the hospital, the voices and people he passed in the reception area, the staff in white jackets that blazed by him as if he were a ghost haunting the hallways.

He found the elevator, felt his body pick up momentum, his heart pounding with fear. What if Christian was alive and coming to take out Nicole? When he stepped onto the floor and saw Jesse down at the end of the long corridor he let out a long sigh. Perched outside her sister's room, keeping a close watch on who came and went, she probably hadn't moved in hours — prepared to remain for as long as it took. He admired the hell out of her for it.

She jumped up as he approached, his uniform filthy, blood stained.

"I've been so worried," she uttered and gave him a hug.

He didn't know where to begin. "How's your sister?"

"Much better. The nurses think she'll be released in a few days."

"Is Nicole good enough to travel now?"

Jesse leaned back and studied him with intense eyes. "I suppose you wouldn't ask unless it was absolutely necessary."

He told her the news about Feinstein, the Riker brothers, and Richard Raulings.

"If he's alive, he knows his older brother's dead. He'll blame somebody. It's the way his mind works. The faster we move her, the better."

"Tell me what I need to do."

He thought it over. "Stay here. I'm going to find a wheelchair."

35

The moorage was as quiet as a graveyard when they arrived. Colefield made a thorough check of the area before he pulled the wheelchair out of the cruiser's trunk and wheeled it around to the passenger door. Jesse climbed out of the back seat and helped Nicole into the wheelchair.

"Jesse, I can walk," Nicole said weakly.

Colefield slung a blanket Feinstein had in the trunk over Nicole's shoulders. "It's a little steep going down the ramp. Humor us, Nicole. Take a ride."

Jesse nudged Colefield aside and took control.

"I remember this lovely moorage," Nicole uttered. "I remember the first day I saw it…"

When they got closer to the ramp, Colefield had them stop while he searched down by the water. They cautiously made their way down toward the houseboats. When they reached the tender, they stopped again. The ramp had a foot gap to get where they wanted to go. The wheelchair had to be lifted. Colefield took the front, Jesse the back and they hefted the wheels up and over the gap and onto the deck. A sensor triggered nightlight came on and lit the narrow path toward Montgomery's houseboat.

Colefield rapped once on his landlord's door and pushed it open. The interior lights were on. Montgomery called out from the galley.

"That you, Old Boy?"

"It's us."

"Good God, it's about time. I've been stewing like a hen."

Colefield stepped aside. "Nicole, we're going to have to jockey the wheelchair inside. I'm going to have you walk in. Can you make it OK?"

"Here, honey, let me help you up."

Jesse stepped to the front. Nicole held onto the large outstretched hands, rose to her feet, and went inside. Colefield followed lifting the wheelchair up the step and into the entryway, closing and locking the door behind them.

He pushed the wheelchair into the salon and had Nicole sit back down. Montgomery hobbled over from the galley using his cane. He had on a tattered blue bathrobe, which Colefield was pleased to see tied shut. His hair was disheveled, wisps of whiteness spurting every which way, but he was awake and eager to help.

"My God, it is good to see you, Ms. Dafoe," Montgomery smiled. He turned and beamed at Jesse. "And who is this lovely creature?"

"Jesse, meet my landlord and friend, William A. Montgomery."

Jesse held out her hand. "Thank you, William. You are too sweet to put us up here."

"The pleasure is all mine," Montgomery said, taking Jesse's hand and kissing it. "Stay as long as you like. I have plenty of hooch and grub and a medicine cabinet better stocked than most pharmacies."

"And an arsenal upstairs in case we need it," Colefield added.

"There is that," Montgomery said, winking. "What can I do to help?"

"Nicole honey," Jesse said, "how are you feeling?"

"I need to lie down."

"Are you in pain?"

"My ribs hurt."

Jesse looked at Montgomery. "She was on Oxycodone at the hospital. You wouldn't happen to have that?"

"Let me scurry off and look."

"I'd like to keep her on the same medication."

"Makes perfect sense."

And with that Montgomery wandered off toward the downstairs bathroom. Colefield could hear him rummaging around in the medicine cabinet. He returned, carrying a prescription bottle. He handed it to Jesse. Jesse turned it over and read the label.

"Perfect," she said.

Colefield walked into the galley and retrieved a glass of water, which he carried back and handed it to Nicole who was eager to wash the pills down.

"Thank you, all of you," she said. "I'm so happy to be out of the hospital."

"And so are we," Jesse put on a fake smile, and then glanced back at Colefield. "Shall I make up a bed for her?"

"It's been done." Montgomery pointed his cane toward the upstairs. "I've changed the sheets and tidied up a bit. It's a bachelor pad so what can I say? There's plenty of room for the both of you. I'll take the downstairs bed. That way I can keep a watch on things, in case we have any unwanted party guests. Now, before either of you retreat to the *chambre principale*, would anyone care for a nightcap?"

Nicole and Jesse shook their heads. "No."

"I'll have theirs," Colefield said.

36

The following day, Colefield got a text from Feinstein to meet him after work at the Sextant. He was also instructed to bring cigars. As Colefield entered the bar, Jill waved him over. "I put your banged up friend out on the back deck."

Colefield looked out the window and saw Feinstein wolfing down a greasy Reuben sandwich, a cigar smoldering on the edge of the plate.

"On your way out," Jill smiled, "you can deliver his next pint."

"Why don't you draw one for me, too?"

As Jill waited for the head to settle she leaned forward and whispered. "That was really sweet and quite a surprise."

"What?" Colefield asked.

Jill untied the bandana knotted around her neck, revealing a gigantic hickey. "Yep — you made me feel like a teenager again."

"What can I say? I have poor impulse control when I see you naked?" Colefield shrugged.

"Obviously, you haven't checked out your own ass. Apparently, I suffer from the same disorder."

Laughing, Colefield picked up the beers and headed to the deck.

"So much for the diet, hey Harv?" He dropped the beers on the table.

"Getting blown up gives a person a new perspective on life. I'd rather die a happy cigar smoking fat man than a skinny sour puss."

"I'll drink to that." Colefield laughed and sat down.

"I think I have finally gotten the entire Dante's inferno business sorted out." Feinstein slurped his beer.

"Start at the beginning."

"When I arrived, the place look deserted. The back door was unlocked. I went inside. It smelled like chemicals and gunpowder and week-old junk food. I hear voices shouting in another room. Probably the brothers ... but before I can do anything, I'm clipped from behind."

"The River Rat?"

"Bingo. He pulled me out of harm's way. When I came to I was propped up where you found me." Feinstein puffed on his cigar. "James was out in the front yard waving his arms around like a lunatic and he's got explosives strapped to his chest. He's screaming Christian's name."

"James spotted me by the tree and told me to keep my distance. I try to get him talking. I throw out some questions about Zoey. Turns out he had a thing for her. When I asked why he killed her, he turned white as a ghost."

"Go on…"

"Turns out the administrator that got attacked in the parking lot, cut off James' benefits. That tipped Christian, his younger brother, off the deep end."

"Christian admitted that he killed her?"

"His brother doesn't know if he meant to kill her or not. It all started there. Zoey saw the whole thing from the woods where we know she liked to go to drink. Apparently, she shared it all with the group. Christian probably figured she could ID him. After that last session, your doctor friend probably approached you, worried about her safety. I don't know what she did with the information."

"I spoke with her boss, Dr. Rosin. She said Nicole wanted to talk to her about something important before her accident. I'm sure she would have mentioned Zoey's confession, especially after the administrator's assault. What about the explosion?"

"Poor bastard," Harvey shook his head. "I don't know if he meant to do it or if the explosives were just unstable and went off."

"And then he became the next victim," Colefield said. "You think James was involved in the killings?"

"Just those he did in Afghanistan."

37

On a sunny Saturday in July, two quiet weeks from the day Jesse and Colefield spirited Nicole from her hospital bed, Jesse decided it was time to throw a much-deserved party. Colefield wasn't so sure. He understood that Nicole was eager to get back to her life and was cleared by her doctor to return to work the following week, but he was still concerned about her safety.

The police reports were in, James Riker was dead. Those had been his body parts and only his at the scene. Christian Riker's blood had also been found, but no one had recovered a body. Colefield figured Christian had met up with Raulings. He believed Riker was still alive and holed up somewhere. His Hummer had not been spotted.

Montgomery told Colefield he was being overly protective. It was time for the girls to live a little. There were always going to be plenty of lunatics to deal with. And he willingly agreed to host the shindig because he had the hot tub. And how could you enjoy a party, he pontificated — if it didn't involve a little nudity?

Montgomery's invited guests from the moorage began trickling in with party favorites and armloads of snacks. And since Colefield had taken the weekend off, he volunteered to work the grill. He'd called Jill extending her an invitation. But she had to work a double. To his surprise, she'd said that if she wasn't too tired afterwards she might stop by. He felt their turbulent relationship had turned a corner.

Jesse had made friends with a new hair stylist who'd asked if she could bring along a friend visiting from out of town. She promised they'd liven things up. When they arrived wearing bikinis it delighted Montgomery.

Sharon and Cheryl were their names. Sharon had the trademark Bettie Page bangs and a curvaceous body. Cheryl was pint-sized with spiky platinum hair. Her look was exotic, sporting an array of colorful tattoos cascading over her shoulders and down to her wrists. They had brought along two bottles of champagne which they passed to Colefield who had walked into the galley to get a fresh beer. Jesse greeted her friends while Colefield opened the champagne and poured each of them a glass of bubbly.

Nicole told Jesse she would be right back and left. She returned a few moments later escorting her boss. Dr. Rosin looked like a different person in casual attire.

Montgomery pulled down a silver goblet from a glass-rack above the stove and held out his pitiful empty rum glass and winked at him.

"Be a good lad, Old Boy, and bestow me with my daily ration."

"The woman over there is Nicole's boss."

Montgomery glanced toward the door for a moment. "She's too old for me. I'll nibble on those young morsels. My, my, I say — this shindig is turning out to be fit for a king."

Colefield had noticed a box of ammo under the picnic bench by the back door. "What's in the ammo box?"

"A gift, Old Boy."

Colefield eyed the bottle of rum on the counter. "Please do us all a favor and keep the ammo away from the barbecue."

Montgomery reached for the Pusser's bottle and proceeded to fill his goblet. Colefield stared at the bottle. Someone had applied a red dot sticker to the label.

"What's with the red dot?"

"Your good doctor put it there. Said it would protect me from evil. She stuck 'em all around the place before she and Jesse moved next door. There's one on my work bench and one on the pearl handle of my .38."

Colefield heard what sounded like water running upstairs. "Are you're filling the hot tub?"

"Does a bear shit in the woods?"

"Who's keeping an eye on it?"

"Lad, I have it under control. How much time before we eat?"

"An hour or so."

"Perfect. I can get a pleasant buzz beforehand."

Nicole walked over from the other room and joined them. "I just wanted to thank you both again for all you've done. William, it was very sweet of you to let us stay with you."

Montgomery's face lit up like a cherry bomb. "It was my pleasure my dear, my bed is your bed, as they say."

Montgomery spotted Jesse across the room and batted his eyes at her. She in turn blew him a kiss. "I'm rather smitten with your sister."

A shadow of a smile crossed Nicole's lips. "And we're both taken with you. Now I think I've about used up my moment of gratitude, so I think it's time to start drinking."

"Splendid," Montgomery said. "The good bartender here will be happy to ply you with liquor."

Montgomery headed outside, leaving them alone.

"I need to show you something." She held out a newsletter that her boss had just given her. "Look at this — let me know what you think."

The front page had a story about her. It mentioned her by name, mentioned the party, who was hosting it, and where.

"Who gave them the information?" Colefield asked.

"I sent some party invitations to the VA. I never dreamed they would publish it."

"Do they send this out to veterans?"

"To some. They also have them scattered around the hospital for people to read."

Colefield frowned. "I see you've been applying red dots again?"

"I sense trouble and see danger ahead."

"If I were being counseled by you, what color would my file have?"

She thought that over. "Red."

"That puts me in the same category as Montgomery?"

She smiled.

"So how long is Jesse staying?"

"She's staying through the summer."

"That's good to hear."

They looked at each other and their eyes locked. Colefield felt the familiar attraction but held back. Nicole studied his expression as if she was trying to read his thoughts. She touched his shoulder affectionately and then went outside to join the others. Colefield stood there staring down at the newsletter, thinking it probably needed a large red dot.

After dinner, the drinking kicked into high-gear. A few more people trickled in from the moorage, saying they'd heard loud music and laughter out on the deck and figured Mr. Montgomery wouldn't mind a few uninvited guests crashing the party.

Across the room, Colefield looked to see if Jill was one of the new arrivals. He didn't see her in the crowd but he did spot Montgomery leading Jesse and Cheryl upstairs toward the hot tub.

Out on the deck, a light, warm breeze was blowing in off the river. It was a perfect night for a shindig.

Colefield wondered where Nicole had run off to. He glanced over at her place. He saw a soft light in her bedroom window.

She had been given a second chance. He thought about the day he and Montgomery had broken into her place. It seemed like an eternity ago.

As he walked away, some loud playful laughter spilled down from the balcony.

Colefield took the last of the raw hamburger from Montgomery's refrigerator to feed Calico Jack.

When he turned the corner he saw Jill standing there. She had a partial six pack of Heineken in hand.

"Am I too late?" she said, setting the beer down on the counter.

"The party's just getting started."

38

He couldn't sleep, just laid there, thinking about the newspaper article and staring at the luminous red glow of the alarm clock, Jill snoozing beside him.

A noise that at first sounded like Calico Jack prowling around outside caught his attention. He sat up. His bedroom backed up against Nicole's place. Only a few feet divided them.

The narrow passageway that ran between the houseboats, the normal haunt for raccoons or stray cats, wasn't the source of the commotion. No, this sounded different. More like a scraping sound.

Colefield crept from bed, careful not to disturb Jill, slipped on some shorts, and grabbed his Glock from a holster hanging on the back of the door.

The breeze had died down to a whisper of warm air against his chest. He slipped along the side of Montgomery's houseboat until he reached his deck. The area was deserted. He checked both ways. Nicole's house was quiet. Shrugging to himself, he started to head back toward his tender.

And then he heard the noise again. This time he noticed the ammo box that had been by the picnic bench was gone. And there were wet footprints leading from the bench toward the water.

He turned around and stared out at the river. No engines puttering by or the whooshing of paddling from a canoer or kayaker. All was quiet on the Willamette. And nearly all the lights were off in the moorage.

Colefield was convinced it had not all been in his head. Proof was there — the wet footprints and the missing ammo box.

And only one person came to mind. The River Rat had come for his goods.

Smiling to himself, Colefield headed back to bed, when a shadow passed between the houseboats. Crouching low, Colefield froze.

A figure emerged onto the deck, his back to Colefield, a tool belt strapped to his waist. Colefield noted the crow bar in his hand. A noise on the river startled the intruder and he looked out over the water, lighting his face in profile. It was Riker.

Colefield remembered his promise to the security guard at the VA. No jail sentence acceptable. If he had to be the executioner, then so be it. But he would inflict pain first — plenty of it.

He was tense and fired up. Then he saw the bastard start to inspect Nicole's door. Standing and moving forward, Colefield swung his gun-hand toward him. But he had underestimated the guy's instinct and speed. Riker dropped the crowbar, lunged forward, tackled him to the ground, and sent his gun flying off in the distance.

Colefield kept his fists up but the blows felt like a ten-pound hammer. He fought back, got in a few solid licks, split open his forehead. He was tough. Riker pulled a tactical knife from his boot.

He swiped the blade in front of Colefield's face, backing him to the water's edge.

"You killed two unarmed women and allowed your brother to slaughter himself. There's got to be a special place in hell for you."

Riker lunged toward him. He sidestepped the knife. A light sliced across the deck as Montgomery's slider opened. The old man hobbled out the door, made a sharp turn to the edge of the deck, not acknowledging the combatants in the dark. He grabbed his dick and started talking to it: "Come on, soldier get the job done." Urine began dribbling into the water.

It was just enough time.

Montgomery suddenly turned toward the men and squinting raised the 410 he held by his side and pumped the gun.

"This the bastard who hurt Nicole?"

But the old marine's reflexes weren't quick enough and Riker made a move toward Montgomery. Colefield grabbed Riker's crowbar and aimed it at his legs. *Make him suffer...*

It was then that Colefield glimpsed a dark figure rise out of the water wielding a .22 pistol, a suppressor attached to the barrel. He fired two quick rounds into Riker's back. The impact barely had an effect. Colefield wondered if the bullets had even hit their target. He didn't see any blood. There was none on him either. He kept staring into the man's eyes for any sudden movement, zeroing in on the knife. If he'd been shot, it wasn't showing. Colefield swung and connected with Riker's knees, and then the man's legs collapsed out from under him. He slid down, still clutching the knife.

Colefield started for the man's weapon. But before he could grab it, Raulings was out of the water and grabbed a patch of Riker's thick hair, slid his bowie knife under the man's throat, and with a powerful quick slice through the jugular, they both slid silently into the black river.

39

The yellow house was located just off Mississippi Avenue, in an area that had once been plagued with gangs, violence and drugs until gentrification moved in. The price of real estate had tripled and the area was hip now. And it came as no surprise to Colefield that the fortyish woman who opened the door had a groovy sort of look.

She had a kind face beneath a floppy hat and rainbow sundress. She wore leather sandals and just enough beads and silver jewelry to give her a little music when she opened the screen door.

"Hello, deputy," she said in a friendly voice. "Mitch is around back. Follow me."

She descended the stairs and led Colefield along a cobblestone path toward the backyard. There were flowers everywhere: roses, mums, carnations, a trellis of bougainvillea, and a small garden where someone had planted a variety of vegetables and herbs.

The yard was small, devoted mostly to the garden. They rounded the back of the house where there was a second garden of several neat rows of marijuana plants. A young man was down on his knees getting ready to plant another seedling in the fresh soil.

"Mitch, look who came to see you…"

The manic teen he had encountered on Lemon Island, chased down the river on a run-away Jet Ski, and eventually turned over to the paramedics, was a changed man.

He stood up and put out his hand. "Mom said you were going to stop by."

Colefield shook the young man's hand, and then looked down at the fresh starts, counting their numbers out aloud. "A little late in the season to be planting them outdoors, isn't it?"

"I'll move them to the basement when the cold weather hits."

Mrs. Steves said, "I'm going to leave you two to yourselves."

Mitch handed Colefield the spade. "Why don't you plant the last one?"

Colefield squatted to his knees. He dug a fair-size hole and Mitch handed him the final plant. He held it for a minute, smelled it, and then set it inside the hole and filled the hole back in with dirt.

Mitch sat down in the grass and faced him. Colefield said, "I can't tell you how long it has been since I planted anything. I'm usually on the other end of the food chain."

"Mom and dad are big on gardens. They're both artists and they taught me the value of working with my hands. Mostly it helps me with my mental state."

"How's that going?"

"I'm not crazed any more. I feel a little sluggish because they haven't got the dosage on my meds right yet. But my doctor says that will ease up in a few weeks. Thanks for not pressing charges by the way."

"I wanted to let you know that I found the guy."

"The River Dude!"

"He's a former soldier. You were right, he witnessed the accident and saved the woman's life, in fact he saved my life, too."

"I told you. He's a super hero."

Mitch picked up some plastic markers and a felt-tip pen and neatly wrote down the strains of each marijuana plant. "This goes with yours."

Colefield took the marker, read it, and stuck it in the soil.
"Girl Scout Cookies, huh?"

"The one to your right is Sweet Tooth. The one next to it
is Mango Kush, and this one is Sour Diesel."

The plants looked the same to Colefield. "How do you tell
them apart?"

"Smell mostly. But there are some subtle differences."

"What're your plans for the rest of the summer?"

"I'm applying for college. Mom thinks I can get a grant."

"Sounds like good advice."

Colefield gave him back the spade and stood, brushing dirt
from his knees.

"When this stuff blooms, you want any of it?"

Colefield laughed. "I'll keep you posted."

Mitch followed him to the front of the house. "I don't
hear voices anymore."

"I probably shouldn't tell you this, but I think it might
make a lot of sense to you. When I was in the Navy, I was out
at sea one night and I heard what sounded like voices out in
the middle of the Atlantic. We were heading toward Europe. I
was on watch. I'd been up for what seemed like days. The
voices were as real as any I've ever heard. Sounded like a man
calling out to his young sons. It was disturbing. But I never
told anyone about it. I kind of had an idea of the coordinates,
so when I got back to port I looked up shipwrecks that had
occurred in that area. There was a cruise liner that had been
traveling from New York to Paris a few years ago. During the
voyage two small boys and their father went missing. It was
presumed that the boys fell in and the father dove in to save
them. But no one knows for certain because there were no
witnesses. Sometimes there are explanations for events that at
the time make no sense."

40

A few days later Colefield had finished up his shift earlier than normal and figured he had a couple hours of sunlight left, plenty time to get in a little fishing.

It was a warm and beautiful evening with the sun just above the tree-line across the Willamette River. He sat down in his favorite lounge chair on Montgomery's deck and cast his line out into the calm water. He cracked open a beer, sat back and relaxed. After a few minutes, Montgomery hobbled out onto the deck and slid a chair over next to him and plopped down.

"Where's your rod?" Colefield asked.

"What?"

"You're rod, where is it?"

"Where it belongs, in my pants."

"So, you're putting all the pressure on me to catch dinner?"

"It's either that or I'm upping your rent."

Montgomery glanced over toward Nicole's place. "Have you seen the honeys?"

"I haven't. I think they went to the coast this weekend. You want a drink?"

"Thought you'd never ask," Montgomery said. "I haven't seen your little mermaid Jill since the party."

"She's on her way over as we speak."

"I never thought you'd have a second chance with that one. You're one lucky sailor."

Colefield let those words swirl around for a moment. He knew just how lucky he'd been. He leaned over and opened the cooler. He took out a cold one. His grip was tight and firm, steady as a rock. He popped the cap off and handed it to his landlord. The old guy looked more relaxed than he'd seen him in some time. His cagey eyes weren't roaming the decks searching for action. He seemed content to just sit back, stare out at the river and watch a small group of kayakers paddle by — no submachine gun at his side, no ammo boxes lined up under the picnic bench, no sniper rifle slung over his shoulder.

They had both come out of this changed...

"So, you tracked down our friend yet?"

"He's moved on."

"Well, he was a good customer, your River Rat. I'll miss him."

"By the way, what was the last ammo recipe you made him?"

"I called them 'Fat Man'. They pack plenty of zing and do massive damage, just like the atom bomb it was named after."

"The medical examiner who picked the lead out of Riker said he'd seen nothing like them before. As soon as they entered the body, they mushroomed out as big as sunflowers, lost all velocity, but destroyed his insides. That's why there were no exit wounds and why I'm standing here today to tell you about it."

"I think you're underestimating yourself, old boy. Don't think for a minute I haven't noticed you've been going through a rough spell. It was called Battle Fatigue in my day. But the symptoms haven't changed. I still deal with my own."

"I'm better now."

"Course you are. You didn't back down from the fight."

"I hope you don't mind but I put an old footlocker in your house. It was Rauling's."

"I nearly tripped over it. It's filled with a bunch of damn newspapers. Why did you bring it here?"

"Each one has an obituary of a fallen soldier. Many of them committed suicide after they were discharged. Over the years, Raulings collected them. All the men who served with him are listed inside. It's all he has left of his comrades."

"Why give them to me?"

"I figured you are best suited to stand watch. Who knows, maybe Sergeant Raulings will show up here again someday and you'll have a chance to give them back."

-- THE END --

ACKNOWLEDGMENTS

Writing takes a team effort, and I have one of the very best. I owe many thanks to my devoted group of first readers who have over the years stuck with me without complaint to the very bitter end. I may have plied them with liquor and gifts to keep them going but it was worth it. Many of their views were taken to heart and implemented in this book. I'd like to give them a big applause: Bill Ashworth; Lee Anna Bennett-Ashworth; Dr. Stephen J. Hanns; Dave Huitt; Kat Majors; Bennett McGough; William A. Montgomery; Lenny Perrone; Harley L. Sachs; Dane Stanich; and a very special thanks to writer Bill Johnson. I was honored to have his help again on this project.

I'd also like to thank all of the independent bookstores and libraries, especially Multnomah County Library, that stock my previous books (and that I hope will add this book to their shelves) and for inviting me to do readings and signings.

I also owe another thumbs up to Multnomah County River Patrol. *River City* and *River Rat* wouldn't have happened without their and Deputy Jason Tyrus' willingness to show me the ropes of what life is like on the River Patrol. They kindly took me out on the water for the real deal adventure as they policed Portland's "Liquid Highways". Hopefully once again my broad descriptions of the River Patrol Headquarters, its procedures, and of the team of dedicated officers who keep the waterways a safer place will meet with their approval.

Finally, thank you to my beautiful and talented Birdie, my fearless partner in crime. Her re-writing efforts ignited my manuscript and shot this novel to life. Without her, I would just be another lonely River Rat, a Whaler of Words. She's the best first mate a captain could ever ask for....

River Rat was written aboard the *Enterprise* in Portland, Oregon.

ABOUT THE AUTHOR

Doc Macomber is a native Northwesterner. His previous books include: *The Killer Coin*, *Wolf's Remedy*, *Snip*, *Riff Raff* – a finalist in the Killer Nashville Claymore Award, and *River City*, a Silver Medal Winner in the 2015 Benjamin Franklin Awards from the Independent Book Publishers Association in the Mystery/Suspense category. Doc served twenty years in the USAF and USANG and formerly served in a Special Ops unit in Portland, Oregon. He currently lives aboard a trawler in the Pacific Northwest. As a decorated Marine Captain once noted, "Doc sees much ... says little ... and writes it all down."

(Author photograph by Ty Hitzemann)

Discover other titles by Doc Macomber

(The Jack Vu Mysteries)

The Killer Coin

Wolf's Remedy

Snip

Riff Raff

(The Jason Colefield Mysteries)

River City

River Rat

(Visit your favorite online retailers to purchase paperback versions, audiobooks, or MP3s.)

Connect with the author online:

I appreciate you reading my book! Please consider writing a review at your favorite online retailer.

Thanks again!

Doc Macomber

(To learn what Mr. Macomber is up to next, visit his website @ www.docmacomber.com)

www.ingramcontent.com/pod-product-compliance
Lightning Source LLC
Chambersburg PA
CBHW021220260626
47172CB00002B/530